TYLER MICHAEL

APEX

Cover Designed by Astrid Burke

First edition

ISBN: 978-0-578-78199-0

This book was professionally typeset on Reedsy.
Find out more at reedsy.com

For WMJ

I

Mobilize

Chapter 1

The trek had become increasingly difficult with each ascending step. The relatively flat terrain in the morning was a good warm-up, but the afternoon was proving more challenging than initially expected. Though the trail was a gradual climb that wrapped around the mountain, the day's effort was beginning to take its toll on the crew. It didn't help that the rains from the night before made their planned river crossing impassable. As the water fell upon the mountain and made its way to the valley, small streams found their way to the main river, transforming it into a treacherous swell that would make even the most ambitious rapids expert think twice.

Chris knew these situations weren't uncommon and that it wouldn't be a true excursion without a few surprises thrown into the mix. Regardless, the new route added three miles to their hike, all of which was a gradual uphill climb. The trail was surrounded with moderately dense forest, which provided a nice shield from the sun but required the crew to keep their eyes down, focused on the multitude of tripping opportunities the root systems had placed in their way. Looking back at the crew, Chris knew they were running short on time; the sun would be down within two hours, and they were at least three from the next camping outpost. They could probably make it shortly after dark, but looking back at Kate and Kevin, who were beginning to fall behind pace, Chris knew it wasn't going to happen.

Chris stopped and turned back to Kate and Kevin. "Alright, guys, we're probably not making it to camp tonight. Sun will be down in a few hours anyway, so there won't be much of a view."

Kate sighed. "Are you sure we can't make it? I don't mind hiking in the dark for a little while. We've done it before."

"True, but at this point in the evening, who knows if they even have any spots left. I was up here a few weeks ago, and the place was filled by about this time..."

"Why didn't we plan a route that would have gotten us there by now?" Kevin interrupted.

"I did, but our planned crossing was significantly deeper and had a much stronger current than expected," Chris shot back. "This was the best route we could take, given the current situation. I think it's best that we start looking for a relatively flat area next to the trail and set up camp."

Kate and Kevin nodded, and the crew continued down the trail. The nearby terrain wasn't dense in shrubbery or small plants, but finding a flat opening near the path that was free of trees and growth was another story. The park allowed for makeshift camping spots as long as no fires were started and campers left nothing behind. Chris was confident they would be fine as long as a sufficient opening could be spotted before the sun went down.

Abruptly, Chris halted pace, went over to the side of the trail, and looked out into the forested terrain. Kate arrived at his side and tried to identify what he was looking at without asking. They quietly waited along the edge of that trail as Kevin brought his saunter to a halt; in the mere fifteen minutes since their last stop, he had already fallen several paces behind.

"Are we there yet?" Kevin asked as he bent over to catch his breath.

"No, but I think I found something we should take a look at," Chris responded as he removed his pack and walked off the trail into the surrounding forest.

Kate followed.

Kevin looked up at the trees. He wasn't a camping expert, but he knew they were running short on time. *Where the hell are they going? Oh well, might as well enjoy a few minutes with this pack off my shoulders.* Kevin followed.

Briskly walking between the trees and brush, Chris and Kate approached a series of bushes clustered next to a large maple tree. Stepping closer, small branches covered with orange, red, and yellow flowers took form, each scaling a thicket next to several trees. Chris approached the bushes, bent down, and carefully examined them.

"Alright, do either of you know what this is?" Chris asked as he gestured toward the flowers and turned to Kate and Kevin.

Kate stared at the bush and then back to Chris and shook her head.

Chris looked to Kevin. "Any ideas?"

"I'm guessing you're about to tell us," Kevin responded in a frustrated manner.

"Hey, you both asked me to help you learn more about how to survive out here. Kate, I know you've been doing this for years, and Kevin, I know this is only your... what? Second? Third?"

"Second."

"Right, well, this one is a nice find." Chris turned and pointed to the bush. "These are jewelweed, they're native up here, and they're safe to eat." Chris quickly removed several flowers. Holding them in his fist, he opened his hand to show Kate and Kevin.

"They've disintegrated," Kevin remarked, peering down at Chris' hand.

"Yes. These plants are frequently referred to as touch-me-nots because they immediately release their seeds once disturbed." Chris reached down with his other hand, took a pinch of seeds from his palm and placed them in his mouth. "Taste similar to walnuts. You can also

5

eat the flowers," he continued. "Either of you like to try?" Chris held out his hand.

"I'm alright for now," replied Kate, who had previously tried similar plants with Chris on more than one occasion.

Kevin shook his head. "I'm really not trying to be a pain, but can we please find a camping spot and then cook some real food? I really need to rest for a few hours."

"Suit yourselves. There's always insects." Chris turned and started walking back to the trail where they'd left off.

Chris, Kate, and Kevin were on the trail for another mile before Kate spotted a plot to set up camp. The site was unremarkable: a gap between a few trees, roughly twenty square feet, that had clearly been used in the past as a pitstop. Chris immediately began unpacking, and Kevin and Kate followed.

"Kevin, do you want me to set up the tents or get moving on food? Your call." Chris gestured as he began to open his pack.

"I'll set up the tents, and you do the food. Fast. Please," Kevin replied as he whipped his pack off and took a deep, exasperated breath.

The camp setup was relatively simple. Kevin had a tent in his pack for himself. Kate had a second, which was large enough for her and Chris. The cooking equipment and food fell to Chris to carry. The goal was to keep each person under forty-five pounds in weight; it wasn't perfect, but Chris had hoped the food and cooking supplies would bear a bit more weight than the camping gear.

The camp came together within fifteen minutes, and Chris prepared a relatively quick meal: dehydrated pasta with some granola he had brought along. He had always hated the prepackaged meals but understood they were the best option when collecting food wasn't the primary objective of the trip. Truth be told, Chris found this particular weekend to be one of the easier ones of the past few months. Kate was an old friend, about to start her second year of business school, and had camped with him many times before. She was very capable in survival situations, as Chris had observed during numerous encounters. She clearly had no need for the current "survival" trek the crew was on, but Chris guessed she just needed a weekend away with a familiar face or two.

Kevin was a different case entirely. A descendent of Korean immigrants, he spent most of his childhood and adolescence living in Silicon Valley parked in front of a computer screen. His overall skills were unremarkable when compared to the broader pool of gifted prodigies in the Valley, but he was more than capable. Kevin studied computer science at Berkeley and was set to graduate next May. The swath of internships and opportunities, though exactly what he wanted, didn't allow for him to disconnect. Kevin spent the summer working for an e-commerce startup. He was part of a team assigned to develop new algorithms that assign a numeric value to each action an individual made on the web. Progress was grueling, results were promising, but Kevin knew this wasn't something a group of interns were going to solve over the summer, especially not without more data. Wrapping his work in early August, Kevin decided to disconnect from the modern world and explore one he didn't grasp. Two weeks later, he was in the Northeast and on his second camping excursion with Chris.

Making quick work of the tents, Kate and Kevin came over to Chris, who was wrapping up the evening's meal. The sun had recently set, and darkness was beginning to take over the camp and surrounding woods. The crew quickly ate their meal in silence as they attempted to refuel from a hard day of hiking, while also looking forward to the prospect of lying down for a few hours.

Shortly after dinner, Chris walked around the camp and grabbed all of the crew's wrappers and unused food containers, and put them in a small yellow sack. "Alright, before we call it, somebody needs to go out and hang this."

"I can do it," said Kevin as he stood. He had learned during his last trip that food and wrappers needed to be stored away from the camp and high in the air, in the event predators or scavengers decided to descend upon their camp. Kevin took a rope and the bag from Chris, and set out down the trail.

Kevin knew he only needed to walk a few hundred feet and then find a solid branch to anchor the pack. After a few minutes, a suitable tree came into view on the path with reasonably low branches from which to throw the rope over and raise the food into the air out of animals' reach. Bears were relatively rare in these parts, but hanging food at a safe height away from camp was one of the must-dos Chris had taught Kevin. As he attempted to throw the rope over the lowest branch, a crackle from down the trail broke his concentration. Pausing, Kevin looked down the path at the glow of a headlight approaching him.

"Evening, any idea how far to the next outpost?" the approaching man inquired.

"At least an hour out if you follow the trail. Sorry, we didn't make it ourselves. One hell of a day," Kevin replied.

"I hear that," the man said as he raised his safari hat, gave his head a quick scratch, and then put it down. "Any chance you know a place where I could set up shop for the night?"

"We might have some extra space at our camp," Kevin said as he gestured for the man to follow him.

Chapter 2

Chris was no stranger to this particular camping trail. Since graduating from Penn last year, he had decided to take a year off from life and explore the "gravitas" that the unemployed world provided. A finance major, with multiple job offers, Chris had his pick of the litter coming out of school but wasn't eager to dedicate his life to sixty-hour weeks behind a computer screen just yet. The outdoors was his true passion, and he spent most of his college summer weekends tackling all of the hiking trails the Northeast had to offer.

Teaching people how to take their survival skills to the next level sounded like a workable short-term plan. In a few months' time, he'd have some money stashed away, and hopefully have a better idea for what he wanted in life. If not, there was always another summer to share insights with novice campers seeking existential bliss brought about by facing nature head-on.

Hearing steps down the path, Chris turned his attention to the trail. He assumed Kevin must have finally found a suitable tree to hang the food. *I sure hope he remembers where he put our stuff.*

"Who's that with him?" Kate asked as she emerged from her tent while putting on a headlamp. The light was fading quickly and would disappear within the next half hour.

Kate was right; as the footsteps drew closer, Chris could clearly make out chatter. Kevin was with someone. Standing, Chris made his way toward the edge of camp to greet Kevin and the unknown individual. It was very common to come across hikers while on the trail. On any given day, Chris regularly crossed paths with half a dozen hikers in this area. In fact, Chris had been surprised at how unusually quiet the trail had been thus far. He assumed this was due to the heavy rains the night before.

"Evening," Chris said to Kevin and his new companion as they approached the campsite.

"Hi folks, how's everybody doing?" the stranger replied.

"Relatively quiet night; we didn't quite make it to the next outpost," Chris quickly replied as he began to evaluate the new traveler.

"Me too. Kevin here was telling me you might have an extra spot to pitch a tent," the stranger politely replied while gesturing toward Kevin at his side.

Looking over at Kevin, who was smiling in approval, Chris approached the two travelers. "I think there might be some space to the left. Happy to help you, Mr...?"

"Ranger."

Ranger was tall, at least six-foot two but relatively lean, and was sporting an old tan safari hat. Chris looked at Kevin and nodded. "Nice to meet you. I'm Chris, and this is Kate," Chris said as he shook Ranger's hand.

"Appreciate it. I hope I'm not intruding. I can always find a place down the trail..."

"No worries. There aren't a lot of places to set up camp between here and the next post. There should be plenty of space off the back. Come over here." Chris gestured Ranger toward the back right of their camp.

"Hike around here a lot, I take it?"

"Went to school a few hours from here. Have hit this trail my fair share of times," Chris replied.

"Nice, this is my first time up here. So far, so good. Was hoping to make it farther north today, but the rain last night didn't help."

"Same here, we were hoping to take the north trail to the next outpost but had to change things up. The river was a mess."

The two men reached an open spot to the left of camp; it was more than big enough for Ranger to pitch a tent. Chris took a second look at Ranger. Tan but clearly of Eastern European origin, his muscles were well-defined, and Chris surmised he was not a novice camper, though something about his getup was off. A scar ran along the left side of his face from the top of his ear down to the jawline, soft but easily noticeable. Ranger was also older than him, but younger than his father, probably in his early forties. Ranger walked up to the open space and offloaded his pack. Moderately filled, he was probably sporting thirty pounds of gear, Chris guessed, from how the pack hung from Ranger's shoulders.

"Need any help setting up?" Chris inquired.

"No, thank you. But a bite wouldn't be the worst; any chance you have something prepared or some leftovers?"

Chris shook his head. "Kevin just hung up what we had. Not really roughing it, most of what we have is prepackaged."

"No shame in that. Did that for years. Just got bored with packaged meals half-filled with salt," Ranger replied as he pulled contents from his pack and began to assemble his tent.

"There's a handful of plants that give berries and such nearby; that's probably your best bet given our lighting situation."

"That's alright, I'll manage until morning. I'm pretty whipped anyway. I'll just skip supper and call it a night." His tent came together quickly, once he found the pole ends and inserted them into the canvas tracks.

"Need any water or anything? We're probably going to call it," Chris said as he began to turn back to their pitched tents.

"Nope, all good. Appreciate your help."

"Alright. Night." Chris waved politely.

Back at the tents, Kate stood with her arms crossed, waiting for Chris' assessment. "Everything okay?" she inquired.

"Yeah. No big deal. Seems like a nice enough guy," Chris replied as he gestured for Kate to enter the tent first. Chris quickly stripped off his sweaty shirt and hung it on a nearby branch.

Inside the second tent, Kevin was already sprawled across the base and lightly snoring.

Chris looked at Kate and laughed as he zipped the entrance shut behind him.

Chapter 3

Mornings on the trail often came faster than expected. Some campers were night sleepers; others couldn't get past the active silence of the surrounding woods. Chris comfortably slept through the night but awoke to the unexpected smell of smoke. Looking around the tent and then over at Kate, who was still asleep, Chris sat up, unzipped the entrance, and headed out.

Looking behind the tents, Chris quickly spotted Ranger sitting on a log a few feet from his campsite, a small fire crackling in front of him.

"Morning," Chris said as he grabbed his shirt from the night before, slipped it on, and made his way over to the fire. Ranger's tent was already back in his pack, and aside from the fire, Chris saw no trace he had even spent the night with them.

"Hey there. How'd you sleep?" Ranger poked the fire with a small stick. Embers lightly shot into the air and quickly faded.

"You should probably put this out," Chris replied as he arrived at Ranger's side and gestured toward the fire.

"I will in a bit. Need to make some breakfast and coffee first. Want any?" Ranger looked up and smiled.

"No. I mean, this is a national park. We're legally not allowed to start open fires around here."

"I have some stones around the base." Ranger gestured dismissively as he pointed to a series of oversized rocks around the perimeter of the fire.

Still waking up, Chris knew this wasn't an argument worth pursuing. He scratched his head and looked around to make sure there weren't any other campers nearby. "Cup of coffee would be nice."

"Sounds good. Have a seat," Ranger said as he gestured to an open spot on the log.

Chris nodded and took a seat on the log next to Ranger. "Where are you headed?"

"Not sure yet. Definitely up the peak, and then I'll probably double back to the lot. Busy week ahead, was just doing some prospecting for a few days." Ranger smiled, grabbed the coffee pot near the fire, poured a steaming cup, and handed it to Chris. "What brings you out here?"

"I'm out here most weeks. Teaching basic survival skills." Chris blew on the coffee and took a sip.

"How's the current crew?"

"They're fine. I've been out with Kate several times, and Kevin's starting to get the hang of things."

"Do you push them hard?" Ranger poked at the fire, then looked up at Chris.

Chris couldn't sense where Ranger was going with the conversation, but had clearly expressed interest in something Chris could talk about at length for days on end. "Ish." Chris shrugged. "Kate is actually quite good and can hold her own. Kevin still has a few things to learn. I'll probably show them a few survival tidbits as we make our way back down; was hoping to work on crossing rivers with Kevin yesterday, but ended up focusing on scavenging. Can't exactly script trips like these, so I do what I can."

"Got it." Ranger took a sip from his coffee mug. "So, what do you do when you're not out here?"

"Still figuring that part out," Chris replied as he followed Ranger with a sip of his own.

"Aren't we all. Still in college or out playing with the big kids?"

"Finished college last spring. Haven't really figured out what to do next, so I've spent most of my time training people until I get a better idea."

"Nothing wrong with that." Ranger paused and took another sip from his coffee mug. "The world isn't going anywhere. Take it from me, don't rush into something because you're expected to. So many people do the right things for the wrong reasons, and then we all end up with the short straw."

Chris smiled and took another sip from his coffee.

"On that note, I'm guessing this right here is what makes you happy. Hell, I bet if you wanted, you could walk off into the woods right now and be just fine for several days. Am I right?"

Chris knew these woods very well and had camped on his own since he was twelve. "Not a problem."

"Hell of a skill set." Ranger raised his mug to Chris. "But practical in the modern world?"

"Practical for me," Chris replied as he raised his coffee mug to Ranger and took another sip. "And what do you do?"

Ranger smiled and blew again on his mug. "I work for an entertainment company that specializes in unique experiences for wealthy clients seeking to embrace cognitive dissonance."

Chris smirked.

"A mouthful, I'm aware," Ranger continued with a smirk. "Forgive me, it's the English literature doctorate talking."

"One of those people," Chris replied. "So, with your job, are you building itineraries or something for these people?"

"Not quite; my firm designs expeditions for our customers. My clients aren't interested in your run-of-the-mill tourism. They come to my company for something a bit more exclusive. They can't get our product anywhere else."

"African safaris and ice breakers to the North Pole type stuff?"

"Something like that. Legally speaking, I can't provide specifics, lots of nondisclosures and such. But I think you're getting the basic idea."

"Sounds interesting. What's your company called? I might look them up when I get back."

"We're called APEX. You'll be hard-pressed to find anything on us from a public domain, though. We intentionally keep our brand off the grid. Our customers expect a higher order of discretion."

Chris was about to ask another question and paused. Ranger was giving him pretty ominous details, and he probably wouldn't get more out of him. "And business is good, I'm guessing?" He took another sip from his mug.

"Business is very good. I'm expanding my team right now; tough to find the right talent."

"I'll be sure to shoot you my resume," Chris replied with a smirk.

Ranger knew Chris was joking but also a bit curious. "You're exactly the type of person we like to bring in. Educated. Can hold his own. Younger, though we don't openly advertise that to management."

There was a long pause as their eyes met. *What is this guy's angle? Is he seriously offering me up an opportunity? Or was it something else?*

"Who the hell started a fire?" Kate asked as she emerged from the tent and made her way to Chris and Ranger.

"Just doing what we can to break protocol," Ranger replied as he smiled and stirred the fire with his stick.

"Got any more of that coffee?" Kate asked as she sat next to Chris. She knew fires weren't allowed in these woods, but for some reason, Chris was playing along.

"So where are y'all from?" Ranger inquired.

"All over. I'm from the DC area, Gaithersburg. Chris is from Denver," Kate blurted while yawning and stretching her arms.

"Haven't been there in for years, went to school in Philly," Chris interjected. "How about yourself?"

"I was born in Texas, but I'm from all over these days. South America for a while. Just spent a few years in Southeast Asia, that was fun. Nothing beats coming home, though; hoping to stay stateside for the foreseeable future, after this next trip, that is." Ranger nodded and held out the coffee pot one more time.

Chris, Kate, and Ranger sat around the fire and engaged in small talk for several cups of coffee until Kevin made his way over. "What'd I miss?"

"Nothing. Just our plot to kill you," Kate replied.

Kevin shrugged and sat down. "Just make it quick," Kevin yawned back to Kate.

"Mr. Ranger was just asking about some of the topics we were covering on the trip." Chris nodded. "Timing actually works nicely." Chris turned to Kevin. "Kevin, if you're out here on your own, what do you do first?"

Sitting down, Kevin knew he wasn't getting away from this conversation or breakfast until Chris heard what he wanted. "Per the wisdom of our great and powerful scoutmaster, we must first find a suitable water source, then move on to a shelter to keep dry, and food comes third."

"Close enough." Chris smiled. There was a long pause. Kate and Chris continued to drink their coffee, Kevin yawned once more, and Ranger kept his focus on poking the simmering embers at his feet.

"Well, I think I've intruded on you folks long enough, and it sounds like Chris has a busy day planned for the two of you." Ranger gestured to Kate and Kevin as he stood and made his way over to the fading fire. Ranger put his boot into the embers and began to stamp them out. He had the fire out within a few seconds and then walked over and grabbed his pack, which was lying on the ground nearby. "And I want to go left out of here, correct?" Ranger pointed down the trail.

"That's right, follow the trail for a few miles; it ends at the outpost,"

Chris replied. "Watch the terrain as you come out of the woods; it's mostly large stones, and you'll need to do some climbing to get to the peak."

"Got it. Sounds fun. Hopefully, I can make it out in time for lunch."

"Shouldn't be a problem," Chris replied. "Appreciate the coffee. Pleasure speaking with you this morning." Chris handed Ranger the empty mug. Kate took a final gulp from her cup and did the same.

"The pleasure was all mine." Ranger smiled, gathered their cups, and headed left down the trail and out of sight.

"Interesting fellow," Kevin said as he made his way toward his tent.

"These trails are full of interesting people," replied Kate. "Some people even tell the truth from time to time." She smiled at Kevin as she made her way back to the tent.

Chris stood. "Alright guys, we have a decent jaunt in front of us today. Let's get packed up and moving." Chris walked over to Kevin. "Dare I ask where you hung our food?"

Chapter 4

The car raced swiftly through the countryside as the sun glistened off its black exterior. The driver's task for the day was simple: bring his passenger to the estate and make haste. After they had spent several hours in close confines together, he had successfully resisted the urge to make small talk or turn on the radio. His employer regarded pleasantries as a nuisance and instructed him to minimize unnecessary interactions; in this, he had not failed. As such, his passenger sat quietly in the backseat, opposite the driver, and gazed calmly out the window.

Rolling hills with trees and the occasional river provided some scenery to help pass the time. It looked like they were driving somewhere through Western Europe, but the passenger couldn't be sure. They hadn't seen another car in over an hour, and he hadn't spotted any towns or villages en route.

It had all come together quicker than he could have imagined. He had been training for this event on and off for the past several months when the phone finally rang. The event was finally in motion, and it was time to make preparations. Of course, they had to pick the weekend he and his wife were at their lodge in the Swiss Alps. The instructions were brief, but everything had fallen into place exactly as outlined. The hardest part was explaining to his wife that he had to leave for a few days; even then, the conversation took all of five minutes. She had grown accustomed to him disappearing for several days on short notice.

The car arrived precisely one hour after the phone call ended. A black sedan with tinted windows pulled upfront. The driver didn't get out or exchange pleasantries when he climbed into the car. By design, he didn't have any bags with him; the instructions on the phone were very clear that everything would be provided upon arrival. The drive was relatively brief, as they made their way down the mountain toward the private airstrip, which was situated in the valley. Mostly used for private charters, it was one of the main reasons he chose the lodge versus others—easy in-and-out access.

The private jet showed up exactly two hours after the phone call ended. Onboard, he was greeted by the unknown man who was now driving the car. The plane was on the tarmac for less than fifteen minutes before they were quickly back in the air and headed toward an undisclosed location.

"Mr. Blue," the driver said as he turned his head toward the passenger. "We're arriving in fifteen minutes."

Is he talking to me? And why now, after hours of silence? "I'm sorry, what was that?" The passenger leaned forward to his right and looked at the driver.

"We'll be at the estate shortly, Mr. Blue."

"Why are you calling me that?"

"That's what I've been instructed to address you as, sir." The driver turned his head back toward the road.

The car continued for a few more miles before the driver began to slow. In the distance, Mr. Blue began to make out a large entrance guarded by a tall metal gate to the left. The car braked and turned to enter. As they rolled to a halt in front of the gate, a tall man in a gray uniform came out to greet them. The driver rolled down the window and exposed a digital watch on his wrist to the guard. The guard pulled out a small black tablet and hovered it over the watch until it beeped.

"All good, sir. Have a nice day."

The driver rolled his window up, and the gates opened. The car proceeded into a wooded area with a small paved road winding through the trees and up a hill.

Mr. Blue's heart rate quickened. The planes, cars, and security were all pretty standard, and he expected some level of sophistication if this event was as advertised. But at this moment, everything felt different than expected. He was finally here after months of training and waiting, and in a matter of hours, he would embark on his first expedition. The company came highly recommended through an unexpected colleague who had recently completed a project of his own. The fees weren't insignificant, but if this experience was half as good as he was promised, it was well worth the investment.

The car broke through the tree line, and on the hill, Mr. Blue caught his first glimpse of the estate.

We're definitely in Western Europe.

The estate sat at the crest of the hill, surrounded by open fields on all sides. The structure was massive and built entirely of stone, at least from the outside. The estate was likely seventeenth century, though Mr. Blue could tell it had undergone its fair share of renovations over the years. The main structure sprawled at least the length of a football field and stood well over four stories high, five in the middle by what Mr. Blue presumed was the main entrance.

The vehicle continued forward. The road curbed into a large circle, which was to be expected. The car slowed as it approached and then came to a stop. Outside the vehicle, a stone staircase rose several feet to two enormous wooden doors, each of which was at least twelve feet tall.

"Best of luck to you, Mr. Blue. They're waiting for you inside," the driver said as he gestured for Mr. Blue to exit the car.

Mr. Blue emerged from the back-right door of the sedan. He raised his hand over his forehead to deflect the sunlight until his eyes had a moment to adjust. Mr. Blue stood five-foot eleven with proportionate weight for his size. In his late thirties, he still had most of his hair, dark brown and combed over to the right, with some gray around the ears starting to emerge. He had a straight cut jaw and a skinny nose. He buttoned up his coat and walked with confidence away from the car and up the stone stairs.

Short of the last step, the giant doors opened, and a thin, balding man wearing an all-black suit and sunglasses emerged. "Right this way, Mr. Blue. They're waiting for you."

Mr. Blue nodded and entered the estate. He caught a glimpse of the man's earpiece as he walked by. *Pretty tight ship around here, good.*

The entryway was immaculate. A large rotunda with intricate details and craftsmanship on display from every angle. Large spiral staircases from both sides that wound up to the second level. A beautiful Greek statue stood eight feet tall in the middle of the room, clearly trying to mimic Venus de Milo. *In a place like this, that's probably the real thing and not mimicking anything.*

The door closed behind him, and the balding man caught up a few strides later. "Over here." The man in black gestured as he pointed down a hallway to the left.

The two men walked briskly down the corridor. Paintings hung on the walls, most of which portrayed classic scenes, such as the Hunt, where hounds and lords pursued a not-so-lucky target, frequently a fox. Mr. Blue found the art impressive but unremarkable; there was nothing provocative about any of the pieces, but maybe that was the point.

The man in black turned right down a second corridor, and Mr. Blue followed. The hall echoed with each step they made on the polished stone floor. At the end of the hallway, there was a large wooden door. The man in black stepped forward and opened it. "Right inside, Mr.

Blue, and thank you again for choosing us." The man in black smiled and walked away. Mr. Blue gave him a nod and then transitioned his attention back to the opened door.

Mr. Blue eased it forward and stepped inside. Before him stood an expansive library. Bookshelves scaled the walls on all sides from floor to ceiling, which was at least two stories high. Each wall had a rolling bookshelf ladder that covered the entire height of the room. There were three entrances: the one behind him, and two on each side of the room halfway down. The books themselves were predominately leather-bound and appeared very old from where he stood. Surprisingly, the room didn't smell of musty old books. *They must have quite the filtration system in here.*

Mr. Blue slowly stepped in and looked around the room. His attention was immediately caught by a shimmer in the middle of the library. Looking closer, Mr. Blue had to take a second glance to confirm what his eyes were seeing. The center of the room had a giant globe of the Earth, suspended in golden rings, at least five feet in diameter and six feet tall. Dark green and red leather chairs were carefully placed at the corners of the globe. It was then that Mr. Blue became aware he wasn't alone.

Sitting in one of the green leather chairs on the far side was a lanky, younger gentleman, hunched over, reading a large leather-bound book. Mr. Blue didn't want to startle the young man but also decided it prudent to announce his presence. Turning around, Mr. Blue slammed the door closed with a thud that echoed through the library. Slowly glancing back toward the globe, the young man was now looking directly at him. The man didn't stand. *Is that who I think he is?*

Mr. Blue began to make his way across the room toward the globe when a creak from the left wall caught his attention, a second man stood high above on a rolling latter. He peered down at Mr. Blue, and then returned his focus to the shelf. Selecting a green-bound book, he descended the ladder and began to walk over to Mr. Blue.

Mr. Blue got a good look at the second man. Similar in height, more or less, he had at least forty pounds on Mr. Blue, but it wasn't fat; this was a well-built human being. He sported a very well-kept short black beard, with the occasional gray spot, and his hair very short with near military precision. "Sun Tsu's *The Art of War*, fifth century BC. Believe it or not, this is the first edition transcribed in English. Beautiful piece, it's a shame they've left it up on that shelf without any protection. Same with a lot of the pieces in here," the second man said as he smiled and gestured toward the book in his hand. Despite the man's intended pleasantries, Mr. Blue immediately sensed an ominous presence from the second man. There was no warmth in the man's smile.

Looking back at the globe, Mr. Blue observed the younger man still hadn't moved, though he was now glancing over at the two of them. Mr. Blue looked back at the stocky gentleman and smiled. Before having the opportunity to respond, a large creak came from the back middle of the library as one of the doors swung open. Through it came a tall, slender man of African descent. He sported spectacles and an elegant black-and-white suit. He approached Mr. Blue with a proper demeanor.

"I see the two of you are already acquainted. Mr. Blue. Mr. Black," the man said with a nod, extending his hand. "I'm the Broker; if you'd please follow me." He shook both hands, clearly exposing the Patek Philippe nestled on his wrist, gesturing for them to follow as he made his way across the room toward the globe.

The Broker approached the young man sitting in the green chair. "Ahh, Mr. White, good to see you again."

Mr. White stood and greeted the Broker with a firm handshake and rehearsed smile. They were clearly acquainted. It was in that moment Mr. Blue knew the identity of Mr. White. *Son of a bitch, that's the CEO of LTC.* Lexicon Technology Corporation, or LTC, had recently gone public, with much fanfare. Their new invasive health monitoring sensors were all the rage with health-conscious Generation Z consumers. People could track in real-time their vitals, blood composition, and overall metabolic burn. Their products were a real game-changer, or at least the street thought so. Fifteen minutes into their IPO, Mr. White had gone from a relatively unknown CEO to the near top of the Forbes 400. He was now known for his cutthroat management style and an incomprehensible knack for losing his best employees.

The Broker gestured Mr. Blue and Mr. Black over. "Gentlemen, this is Mr. White. Mr. White, this is Mr. Black and Mr. Blue." They all nodded at each other and shook hands. "Now, gentlemen, if you would please follow me," the Broker added as he gestured the three men through the open doors on the opposite side of the room.

Chapter 5

The four men exited the library and headed into the study. Mounted on the walls were the heads of some of Earth's most sought predators: lions, rhinos, elephants, zebras, and hippos. They were elaborately decorated and mounted between the windows along the entire length of the room. Across the back wall, a large fireplace rose from floor to ceiling. The fireplace pit itself was over five feet tall and ten feet wide. Above the pit was an intricate carving depicting the four horsemen of the apocalypse. Old weapons and tools were displayed throughout the room; most were antiques and likely hadn't been used for a century. In front of the fireplace was a large wooden desk.

"Since the dawn of time, man has sought to cement his rule over the land by taking down the world's greatest predators, many of which you see here. Though the hunting of these creatures was originally a means for survival, it's now almost exclusively for sport," the Broker began. "In the nineteenth century, a taxidermist named Rowland Ward became the first to capture and catalog world records of these creatures, and so began a century that saw the methodical slaughter and destruction of habitats all over the world," the Broker continued while pointing at a leather-bound book on a stand to their left. "Today, sport hunting is a multibillion-dollar industry, with many great species facing extinction from overhunting, yet masters of the hunt from all over seek to test the limits of their natural prowess and problem-solving skills." The Broker turned around and looked at the three men. "What we do here takes that concept to the next level. At its very core, what you're about to embark on will be a test of mind, body, and soul. And make no mistake, you will face very real and mounting challenges, and you'll square off against an opponent that is offered nowhere else in the world."

The Broker continued walking through the room, making a direct line toward the desk at the other end. The three men hung back and looked around at the trophies. "Your instructors have informed me that you all cleared basic training, and to confirm, you've each selected our Most Dangerous Excursion scenario, correct?" Quickly turning around, the Broker looked to each person to acknowledge and agree with his statement. Each nodded. The Broker turned back and continued walking to the desk. "Good. We haven't done this scenario in quite some time, but the site is in final prep right now, and we're looking to drop in three hours."

"We're going in right now?" Mr. White inquired in surprise.

The Broker arrived at the desk, walked around, and sat in a large chair at the center. "That's right. And we have a lot to cover. Please have a seat." He gestured for everybody to approach the desk and sit at the chairs in front.

All three men approached the desk and took a seat. The Broker looked to his left and gave a wave. Out of the back corner of the room, a young woman emerged and began to walk toward the group. In her hand she had a large black case.

"This is Paige. She needs to square away a few items with you before we get started," the Broker said as she arrived at his side and carefully set the black case on the desk. With a quick pop, she had the locks open, and the top of the case rose. Inside was a screen and keyboard. Paige was dressed in black business-professional attire; she was on the shorter side with short brown hair, and in her early thirties. Judging by her demeanor, she had been through this exercise on several occasions.

"First things first. Gentlemen, if you would, please empty your pockets and place everything in front of you on the desk. Phones, wallets, smartwatches, anything that isn't clothing," she started.

The three contestants emptied their pockets and put the contents on the table. Leaning into the black case, Paige pulled out three manila envelopes, each marked with names. Turning away from the Broker, she made her away around the desk and handed each person their assigned envelope. "Please place your belongings in the envelope and seal. You'll get these back at the end of the excursion."

The men did as instructed and handed Paige their sealed envelopes moments later.

Returning to the case, she continued by reading off a series of questions. "None of you currently take any medications, correct?"

All three nodded.

"No pacemakers, medical implants, hips, knees, shoulders."

All three nodded again.

"None of you are diagnosed with heart disease, hypertension."

All three shook their heads.

"And I presume none of you are currently pregnant?" she said with a straight face.

All three smirked and shook their heads.

"Thank you." She handed the Broker the sealed envelopes and turned her attention back to the screen in the case, typed for a few seconds, and then looked back at the three men. "I need your fingerprint and signatures on these non-disclosure forms," she said as she twirled the case around and in front of Mr. Black. "Sign here and press here," she added while pointing at the case's keyboard and touchpad.

"Do I need my lawyer?" Mr. Black inquired, and he looked at the Broker questioningly.

"This is our standard non-disclosure form citing you won't disclose any details of this expedition, any events that occur, anything you see or interact with while on location, and any information pertinent to your relationship with our organization," she replied, as Mr. Black continued to look at the Broker.

Mr. Black looked at the fine print in the screen, and then up at Paige with apprehension.

"You're not going out there unless you sign this," she added. "I must also remind you that this agreement is binding for the remainder of your lives and will be enforced."

Reluctantly, Mr. Black shifted his gaze to the case, signed the touch screen, and pushed his thumb into the pad. Paige smiled and moved on to Mr. White and Mr. Blue, who did as she asked without question.

"Great. Next, we have our liability waiver," she said while returning to Mr. Black.

"From what?" Mr. Blue inquired.

"Personal injuries, or death."

"Outstanding," Mr. Black said as he eagerly signed the screen a second time. Mr. Blue wasn't sure if Mr. Black was being sarcastic.

Paige again moved through the group and collected signatures.

"Thank you, gentlemen. Now the fun part," she added, returning to Mr. Black's side of the desk. Pausing, she began to type and brought up another screen. She glanced over the screen and then looked up at the Broker. "Funds are set."

"Thank you," the Broker said while nodding to Paige, who closed the case, smiled, and walked out of the room.

The Broker opened the desk drawer to his left and pulled out a manila envelope. Reaching across the desk to his left, the Broker picked up a letter opener and quickly slit it open across the top seam. Setting the letter opener back in place, he pulled out several sheets of paper from within the envelope and lightly stacked them together on the desk. He quickly fingered through the paperwork and cleared his throat.

"The rules are as follows," the Broker began as he handed a piece of paper to each of them. "Duration is thirty-six hours on-site. You will be delivered via helicopter. The drop zone will be south of the extraction point."

The three men looked down and began to review the paper.

"And, the stakes—" The Broker paused and flipped to the next page. "Buy-in was $17,000,000 each, confirmed via secure transfer. Our fee for this event is twenty percent. That leaves the purse at just under $41,000,000. Game scenario is winner-take-all," the Broker continued. "Scoring is as follows: one hundred points for flesh wound and five hundred for a kill. Points will be granted by our judge panel."

"I thought we were alone out there?" inquired Mr. Black as he looked up at the Broker.

"That you are, but we would never leave something like this to chance. Your prey will be quite capable of adding an element of danger, which, by design, is what makes this a unique experience." He sat silently for several seconds. "You'll be monitored at all times. We'll get to that shortly." The Broker paused to make sure Mr. Black was satisfied. Mr. Black returned his gaze to his handout. "Now, as I was saying, and this is important, time is an asset. To win, you need to make it to the extraction point before time runs out. If you have high score but don't make it to the extraction point before time expires, the prize will be awarded to the highest-scoring member at extraction."

The three men nodded, looking at the Broker and each other.

"In the event of a tie, we will exercise the tiebreaker contingency, which I have sealed here in my desk. We haven't had a tiebreaker in several years, but we are prepared should the scenario arise. There will be a winner." The Broker paused and ensured each of the three men understood. Looking down at his paperwork, the Broker flipped another page. "Now, some of the dos and don'ts. First, no trophies. You make a kill, you move on, and our cleanup crew will take over."

Mr. Blue began to interrupt. "Who would..."

"You'd be surprised by what we've seen over the years." The Broker didn't break pace. "Second, under no circumstances are you to intentionally interfere with another's pursuit. Nor are you allowed to intentionally compromise the safety and/or wellbeing of your fellow members. Failure to do so will result in your immediate disqualification. Intentional bodily harm toward fellow members, in particular, will not be tolerated, and we will step in if necessary. Are we clear?"

The three men all nodded, not making eye contact with each other.

"I need a verbal yes from each of you. Mr. Blue?"

"Yes"

"Mr. White?"

"Yes"

"Mr. Black?"

"Loud and clear. But what of unintentional interference? Say we thought we were alone in pursuit, or we stumble across somebody else?"

"If you can't manage to resolve the situation as adults, we can have a judge rule. You'll each be sent out with a flare gun as part of your pack; if there's a dispute, one of the acceptable uses of the flare gun is to trigger a dispute challenge. Shooting the flare into the air will notify our team that we need a judgment, and somebody will join you shortly to mediate."

"Works for me," Mr. Black quickly replied.

"Third, and this is the last bit of information before we send you over to wardrobe. Once the clock starts, you are on your own. You are not allowed to tap out and call it quits if something doesn't go your way. However, there are two scenarios in which we will get involved. First, in the event of unexpected severe weather, we will suspend play and route you to a service tunnel. Now, before one of you interrupts me again, let me say this: yes, there are service tunnels, this is a highly sophisticated terrain with multiple access points for our team and yourselves. Should we call it on weather, we will route you to the closest access point, all of which will also be marked on your maps."

The Broker paused to see if there were any questions or comments; nobody said a word. "Second, if you are mortally wounded or have a severe medical emergency, you may exercise an opt-out. As I said before, your prey will introduce challenges, and their behavior can be unpredictable." The Broker paused and smiled at the crew for several seconds before continuing. "That flare gun I mentioned a minute ago can also be used to signal for help. Fire it straight up, and an extraction crew will come and assist. Any questions?"

All three remained silent.

"Good, then let's go get your gear."

Chapter 6

The day was coming to a close. Chris, Kate, and Kevin had finally made their way out of the woods and on to flat, open terrain. They'd gotten a late start to their day due to a few challenges in recovering the food sack Kevin had hung the night before. The sack's rope got lodged on a tree branch and wouldn't move. After numerous attempts by Kevin to swat the sack with various downed branches, Kate resorted to scaling a nearby tree and was able to knock it down and help get the crew back on track.

The sun was beginning to set on their second day on the trail. Camp was already set up, and Chris sat hunched over a propane burner with a cooking pan in his hand. The late start to the day had resulted in yet another course correction; instead of going up the mountain, they'd doubled back and descended into the valley. The trek took a lot less time than Chris anticipated, so he brought Kevin and Kate to a nearby lake he had frequented many times before, and they spent the afternoon fishing.

Kevin had the first catch, a beautiful thirteen-inch rainbow trout. Unfortunately, rainbow trout were protected in this state, so Chris had him carefully extract the hook from the fish's mouth and return it to the water. That was the first of two rainbows Kevin caught during the afternoon. Kevin quickly called it a day shortly after his second catch-and-release. Luckily, Kate had better luck and snagged a pair of small-mouth bass.

In the pan, Chris had the fish searing golden brown. Using his water bottle, he sprayed a few shots of water into the pan. The fish sizzled as steam rose from the pan. He lightly shifted it in his hand, slightly moving the fish back and forth to minimize the stick and keep them from burning.

Kate approached and took a seat next to Chris on a nearby log. "How's it coming?"

"See for yourself."

She peered into the pan; the fish continued to sizzle and crack. "Looks good to me."

"Yeah, I think we're good," Chris said as he sat the pan on the ground, reached over to the small propane burner, and closed the valve. The small flame flickered and went out. Chris reached back to the pan, picked it up, and set it between him and Kate. "I only have one fork."

"I'd use my fingers if it wasn't so damn hot."

Chris handed Kate the fork. "When are you heading back to school?"

"Week and a half, I think?" Kate replied as she carved away a chunk of fish from the pan, scooped it on to the fork, blew on it, and then took a bite. She gasped slightly as she chewed the fish. *Hot.*

"And this is year two?" Chris continued.

"Yes. Just finished my internship last week. Will head back to DC on Sunday." She handed Chris the fork.

"Did you get an offer this summer?"

"I did, but I'm not sure CPG is really where I want to spend my time. I learned a lot this summer, but the work was very repetitive, and I think I need something with a bit more pace and change. Maybe a consulting gig," she added.

Chris took a bite of fish, reacted similarly to Kate, and wiped his mouth with his forearm. "Needs to cool down," Chris laughed as he tried not to spit out any of the fish. "But yeah, that makes sense. Are you hoping to stay east?"

"That's the plan right now, but honestly, we'll see what happens. There will be another hiring wave in the fall. I'll probably stay a bit picky the first few months, and then open things up if I don't get the right offer."

"Right on. And how are the parents?" Chris added as he handed the fork back to Kate, who swung and took the fork from him.

Kate broke eye contact and shifted her focus down on the food, clearly agitated. "Mom is down in Richmond. She's well, still living alone. Dad is up in Manhattan. Haven't seen him in over a year, but it looks like he married Meredith. She friended me on Insta, but I'm not quite ready to take that step. It's a bit of a mess. I'm sure she thinks I'm a total bitch."

"I can only imagine. Sorry for asking."

Kate took another bite of fish. "No worries. I'm making it work. Hoping to see my mom before the semester starts."

Kevin walked up with a flask in hand and gave Chris a warm smack. "Smells good. Any left for me?"

Kate was relieved by Kevin's timely arrival. "Only if I can have a swig of that." Kate gestured toward his flask.

Kevin walked over, sat next to Kate on the same log, and handed her the flask.

"Thanks." Kate took a swig with one hand and handed Kevin the fish pan with the other. Kevin dug in and began to heave chunks of fish into his mouth.

"So tomorrow, I'm thinking we wrap around on the Pike Trail, and that'll get us back to the cars by three-ish," Chris began as Kate nursed the flask and Kevin continued to eat.

"How many miles, do you think?" Kevin inquired while still looking down at his food.

"Maybe five, give or take. We don't have to start early, if that's what you're asking."

"Nope, just trying to prepare my body." Kevin laughed. "My legs were Jello today after yesterday's climb."

"You'll get used to it after a few more hikes," Kate added.

Kevin laughed. "This coming from a DI athlete."

"DII." Kate smirked as she took another swig of the flask and handed it back to Kevin empty. "I hope you have more."

***

Chris, Kate, and Kevin sat around the campsite for another hour until the sun was down and then called it a day. Kevin retired to his tent, and Chris and Kate shared again. Similar to the night before, Kevin was out very quickly, and his snoring kept Chris and Kate awake for a little while before they succumbed to exhaustion themselves.

It was five hours after sunset when the soft rumble first made it to their ears. Overall, the night was relatively quiet. The gentle wind moved the tree leaves and brush slightly, and the sound of nocturnal insects dominated the otherwise silent space.

The rumble became louder. Chris slowly opened his eyes to the new sound. *Didn't think it was supposed to storm tonight.* Sitting up, Chris rubbed his eyes and leaned toward the entrance of the tent.

Kate rolled over. "Need help with anything?" she whispered.

"Nah. Just making sure we don't have anything that shouldn't get soaked or could blow away. I'll be back in a second." Chris flicked on his headlamp and unzipped the tent.

Kate rolled over and went back to sleep.

The rumble in the distance grew louder. *The sound hasn't broken; it can't be thunder.*

Chris stepped into the camp. The wind sent a chill up Chris's shirt. *Should have grabbed my jacket.* Chris quickly tip-toed around the perimeter of the camp. Everything appeared in place. Their overall footprint was mostly contained, except a few articles of clothing hanging between nearby trees. Chris made his way over to the line and began to take down the clothes.

The rumble stopped abruptly.

Chris looked around. *Definitely not thunder. Maybe a park ranger, although that doesn't feel right.* Out of an abundance of caution, Chris took down the hanging clothes, quickly folded them the best he could under the light of his headlamp, and quietly made his way back to the tent.

While approaching his tent, a branch snapped in the brush behind Chris. It was very distinct, a branch or stick that was broken by weight or stress. Chris crouched down and looked behind him, gently setting the clothes on the ground next to the tent. *Nothing.* It wasn't uncommon for small animals to investigate campsites. After all, his crew was on their turf, but as hard as he tried to rationalize it, he knew that wasn't right.

Chris flicked off his headlamp and stayed in a crouch near his tent, trying to remain as silent as possible. He glanced at the perimeter of the camp from left to right. Silence. Chris waited another few minutes and carefully watched for any movement. *Nothing.* He took a deep breath and began to shift back toward the tent.

A muffled breath sounded to his left.

Chris immediately darted up and changed positions next to the tent. *Now that was definitely something or someone taking a breath.* Chris turned on his headlamp. *Dammit. Last thing we need right now is a bear.* If it was a bear, Chris knew he had to make noise, and fast, but it would likely wake up Kate and Kevin. He quietly unzipped the front of his tent, reached to the left, and pulled out the pan they'd used for dinner earlier in the evening and a smaller cooking pot. He tapped Kate's leg. She didn't move.

Chris zipped the tent closed and inched forward in a crouch. *Alright,*

get clear of the tent, maybe over by that tree, and then start making noise.
He slowly moved forward and made his way toward a birch tree to his right...

The attack came from his left. Chris was knocked off his feet in a single blow. Gasping to catch his breath and reorient, Chris rolled onto his stomach. As he started to climb up on his knees and elbows, a strong arm came around his neck and put him in a firm chokehold. A voice whispered into his ear. "Shh, shh, shh, easy, Chris."

Chris tried to move and get a glimpse of his assailant. He wasn't strong enough. As quickly as the attack began, a sharp prick pierced Chris' skin from behind his ear, and all went black.

Chapter 7

Mr. White emerged from the dressing room wearing the new garments he had been instructed to try on. Outside the door waiting for him was Captain Miller; they had met minutes before when Mr. White came into the room, and Captain Miller had presented him with his stack of clothing. Captain Miller looked the part of former military: well-built, clean-cut, buzzed gray hair, and a no-nonsense demeanor. Captain Miller began to carefully evaluate Mr. White the second he emerged from the dressing room.

"Lift your arms," Captain Miller said as he inspected Mr. White's fitting. Mr. White complied. "How's it feel?" Captain Miller added.

"A little tight, but overall feels good." The shirt was made of brown athletic wear and felt different from anything he had worn before. The shirt itself was unbranded but was soft to the touch and breathed well.

"It's supposed to be tight. Want to make sure you have a full range of motion." Captain Miller looked down. "Pants fit good, and you managed to put your boots on correctly."

Mr. White nodded. His pants were slim but appeared very durable. They were primarily composed of a dark cedar green material, except at the seams where a dark brown strip ran from the waist to his ankle. There was a single cargo pocket on the left leg just above his knee. On his feet were black-and-brown hiking boots, similar to those he had worn on previous hunting excursions.

"Alright, fall in and join the others." Captain Miller nodded as he followed Mr. White into the equipment room and took position in the middle.

The equipment room was by far the smallest one Mr. White had seen that day, aside from the changing room. Cement walls on all sides with a series of hooks and shelves along the back, composed entirely of camping and hunting equipment. In the middle were three metal tables. Mr. Blue stood behind the leftmost one, Mr. Black in the center, and Mr. White made his way over to the last table. Over Captain Miller's left shoulder, standing silently against the wall, was a young man, no older than twenty, dressed head to toe the same as Captain Miller. He never flinched.

On the tables was an assortment of packs and gear spread across nearly every inch of each surface. "Gentlemen, step forward. In front of you is what you're allowed to bring out in the field," Captain Miller began. "Contents are as follows: one twenty-pound pack, one two-liter water filtration unit..."

Mr. White looked down at the pack. Still empty, but a very unique design. The main pouch was off-center, small pockets on the front, a mesh pocket on the left, presumably for a water bottle, and a large cylindrical compartment taking up essentially the left third of the pack. *Interesting.*

"...One box of matches. One military grade spring-loaded knife with locking mechanism, not to be confused with one of those candy-ass switchblades people have out there. One cooking pot with food rations for four meals; yes they're all dehydrated food packets, and not what you're probably used to, but they're light and don't take up a lot of space..."

Mr. White picked up a compact circular pad with a zipper around the perimeter from the table.

"A compact sleeping unit that will unfold into a cylindrical compartment that can house one body. There's a blanket and inflatable pillow attached. Don't prefer these myself, but will be helpful in protecting each of you from bug bites."

Mr. White nodded at Captain Miller and put the sleeping pack down on the table.

"... Mr. Black, not in here, put that down."

Mr. White looked over at Mr. Black who had his flare gun in his left hand, and the flare round in his right. Mr. Black cautiously set the two items back on the table.

"... Jesus Christ." Captain Miller shook his head and attempted to continue. "As you know, you have one flare gun and one flare round. Use it wisely!"

That was everything on the table. *Simple and to the point,* Mr. White thought to himself. *Feels too simple. Are they really expecting us to hunt with a knife? Do they expect us to build our own weapons?*

Captain Miller walked to the back wall. "Now for the fun part." He reached the end of the room and withdrew a black object from the wall. Roughly a foot and a half long, several inches wide, and appeared to be folded. Returning to the middle of the room, he held the object out, and with a flick of his arm, it opened and locked into place with a snap. It was unlike any model Mr. White had ever seen, but it was clear what Captain Miller was holding – a bow. "Little gift from our friends at Odessa. This darling is called the Black Hawk. Should handle similar to those you've trained with over the past few weeks, with a few customizations, of course. Very smooth, and I like this one in particular because of the shorter draw." Captain Miller walked up to Mr. White and placed the bow on the table. "Locking mechanisms here and here, release is here," he said while pointing to two key hinge spots in the bow.

Stepping back from Mr. White's table, Captain Miller looked over at his young counterpart, who stood silently in position and nodded. The young man made his way to the wall and brought back two more bows.

He brought one to Mr. Blue and Mr. Black, and then returned to the far wall. Opening a cabinet beneath the shelves, he brought out three cylindrical packs, each more than two feet long, and brought them to the tables.

"Why not guns?" asked Mr. Blue. "We trained with several different weapon types."

"Guns are loud," Captain Miller began. "The terrain for this trip carries sound very well. Additionally, with a gun, you can fire far more rapidly. We've found in previous expeditions that contestants tend to be more haphazard in their tactics when using guns, and it resulted in more unnecessary injuries than my superiors were willing to accept. A bow brings balance to the calculus. You'll still have a significant competitive advantage over your prey; I wouldn't worry."

Mr. Blue looked down at the bow, and then disappointedly back up at Captain Miller. "Got it."

"You have twelve shots each. That's it. There's a compartment on the left side of your pack where you can store them." Miller gestured toward Mr. Blue's backpack.

Mr. Black picked up his bow, quickly unlocked it, and swung the ends into position. With a click, he pivoted toward the wall and drew the bow as if he were holding an arrow. He looked over at Mr. White and grinned. Mr. White was here to win, but he knew there was something different about Mr. Black. *Bastard better follow the rules—and stay away from me.*

"You have fifteen minutes to collect your gear, and then we're shipping you back to the Broker. We have one more briefing, and then it's showtime."

Chapter 8

Mr. Black, Blue, and White were escorted to a small conference room that was surprisingly modern when compared to the rest of the estate. The main wall was made of LCD screens that hid nearly every inch of surface. The three men each took a chair at a long rectangular conference table that could comfortably seat a dozen people; they spaced out and kept their distance from one another. The conference room lacked windows and relied on lighting from the panels above. They waited silently, dressed in full gear, with their packs leaning against the wall.

The conference room door swung open, and the Broker walked in carrying a small gray box. Behind him, a second individual followed. The new man was tall and moderately tan, clearly having spent significant time outdoors, and had a small scar on the side of his face. He walked to the back of the table and took a seat by himself. The Broker walked briskly to the front of the room.

Mr. Black glared at the new man as he entered the room and sat down. *Where do they find these guys?*

"We're running a few minutes behind schedule, so let's get started," the Broker said as he set the gray box on the table and opened the lid. Reaching inside, he removed a black smartwatch with an oversized screen and held it up for the room to see. "You're each getting one of these and are required to wear them at all times. They tell us exactly where you are and will enable us to send messages throughout the excursion when necessary. For you, it will keep track of how much time you have left."

The Broker walked over and handed the black watch to Mr. Black. Going to the far side of the table, he removed a blue watch and handed it to Mr. Blue, and finally a white watch to Mr. White.

Mr. Black looked down at the silicon-looking watch and gave it a soft twist. *Whatever this band is reinforced with, it's strong as hell.* Reaching down, he set the watch on his wrist and brought the two ends together. It immediately locked snugly around his wrist with a soft click. Intrigued, Mr. Black pulled at the locking mechanism; it didn't give any slack.

"How the hell do we get these things off?" Mr. Black said as he continued to tug at his wrist.

"They don't come off," replied the Broker. "Not until we take them off." Mr. Black paused and looked at the contestants for several seconds. "Gentlemen, none of you are leaving this room without putting those on."

Looking down at their wrists, Mr. Blue and Mr. White reluctantly followed suit and locked their watches into position.

Satisfied with the group's compliance, the Broker walked toward the front of the room. "Now, let's meet your prey," the Broker said as he pulled up a remote, dimmed the lights, and then turned his attention to the LCD wall, where three profiles flashed on the screen.

Mr. Black smiled and leaned forward to review. *Here we go.*

"First up on the left: Kevin Wu. Age: 21 years. Height: 5'6. Weight: 145 pounds. Studied computer engineering at Berkeley, currently works as an intern for a startup in the Valley. He has limited experience in the wild, zero experience in weapons or hand-to-hand combat training. He's an apt problem solver, though we haven't observed how well his technical skills translate to the wild. We anticipate he will be the most cautious of our prey. His height and weight combination also suggest that he will be a slippery target to hit. We're giving him a prey score of 4.2/10."

Mr. Black sat back in his chair, crossed his arms, and shook his head. *Little pissant doesn't stand a chance. I can't believe I paid $17 mill for this shit.*

The Broker pivoted his attention to the middle profile. "Next, we have Kathryn Alan. Age: 23. Height: 5'11. Weight: 156. About to enter her second year of MBA school at Georgetown and spent the summer in the Midwest working as a CPG operations intern. Formerly a DII track athlete in the 800 and 1600 meter. She's credited with a few regional accolades and is clearly the most genetically gifted of the trio. Furthermore, our assessment is that she is in peak physical condition. Similar to Mr. Wu, background check shows no formal training in hand-to-hand combat, and limited weapons experience as a young adult at summer camps. That being said, her combination of athleticism and outdoor experience should not be underestimated. We're giving Miss Alan a prey score of 8/10."

"What's the protocol on capturing our prey?" Mr. Black inquired with a smirk on his face.

"Jesus. You can't be serious..." Mr. Blue interrupted.

"I'm only playing, Professor," Mr. Black said dismissively. "This is a hunt, not a catch-and-release, or catch-and-keep. Right, Mr. Broker?"

"That's right, Mr. Black," the Broker said as he gave him a stern glare.

There was an awkward silence. Nobody in the room spoke for several seconds.

The Broker continued, "Moving on. On our far right, we have our third and final candidate, Christopher Arians. Age: 23. Height: 5'11. Weight: 187. Studied finance at Penn. He's currently unemployed and teaching camping skills on weekends. Mr. Arians is a former Eagle

Scout and has well over a decade of experience in the field. He is by far the most equipped to handle our current setup and is the leader of our group. There were no records of formal weapons training that we could find, but he was captain of his high school's wrestling team for three years. We're giving him a prey score of 8.7/10."

Mr. Black smiled, leaning forward. *Now we're talking.*

"Gentlemen, these are your prey. Any questions?"

"Seems like a mixed bag of candidates; are you sure you've evaluated them properly? I don't want to get out there and have the game be over in three hours," blurted Mr. Black.

"I evaluated them myself; they'll do well," the man at the back of the room said as he stood. "We've been doing this for years and have progressively refined our methods. Nearly to a science. I assure you that it won't be over in three hours; in fact, I'd wager this goes through until nearly the end." He walked toward the front of the table. "I can promise you that our experience will meet and exceed your expectations." He stopped at the other end of the table next to the Broker.

"Gentlemen, this is Ranger. He'll be moderating the expedition from the ground," the Broker added.

Mr. Black, Blue, and White sat silently at the table. The tension was beginning to mount in anticipation. They had trained for months. Flown in from all parts of the planet. Spent the day in preparation and were on the cusp of engaging.

"Now, if there aren't any other questions, we need to ship out."

"Actually," Mr. Black interjected. "I have one more."

Ranger nodded at Mr. Black.

"I get how we're keeping tally of the score, but Mr. Broker here said that judges would be allocating points. Exactly how many people besides yourself will be out there? Feels like there will need to be many in order to track our activity accurately."

Ranger smiled. "We have minimal staff on location. You won't see anybody the entire excursion, except possibly me. Now, as far as keeping score, the process is a bit more complicated. You all should start by taking a look at your shirt collars."

All three men looked down and tried to glance at their shirt collars.

"Below the rim, center breast. See that shiny dot?"

Mr. Blue and White looked at their shirts, shook their heads, and sat back waiting for Ranger to provide an explanation.

Mr. Black carefully looked down at his shirt collar, and seconds later knew precisely what was on his shirt. Though he rarely worked anymore, he considered himself a technology expert and had allocated significant resources in startup technologies over the years. *5G enabled Nano HDs. They're not supposed to hit the market until next year.* "These aren't supposed to exist yet," he said as he looked up at Ranger.

"Gentlemen, welcome to APEX."

II

Expedition

36:00:00

Inhaling deeply, Kate anxiously woke and sat up in one motion. Her vision was blurred by the sun that had already broken through the tree line in front of where she sat. Kate looked down and used her hand to shield her recovering eyes. She was sitting in a flat patch of long grass.

She felt fine, but something wasn't right. *What happened last night? And where is the tent?* Her vision started to clear, but she kept her hand in place as she stood slowly. Slightly disoriented, it took her a few seconds to get to her feet. She gazed around; a grass meadow swayed softly in the wind, with a tree line in front and behind her. Large hills framed the landscape in the distance.

Quickly looking down, she inspected her body from feet to shoulders. *Still wearing the same clothes from last night.* Looking down at her forearm, she spotted a red watch snug on her right wrist. "The hell is this?" she said quietly to herself. The watch had a digital screen, the band made from some sort of heavy silicon—not plastic or leather, and definitely not cheap. There were no buttons or knobs on the watch face. The screen showed a static number of 36:00:00.

Shifting her wrist around, she inspected the watch from all sides. The material was seamless, with no point to connect or disconnect. Reaching down, she gave the watchband a tug. It didn't budge or show any signs of stress. She grunted as she pulled a second time. The watch didn't give. Realizing it wasn't going anywhere, she shifted her attention back to the field. *Where are those guys?*

Quickly surveying the landscape in front of her, Kate took a few steps forward and then stopped, pivoted ninety degrees, and took another few steps. Everything was out of place. The wind blew gently on her face as her eyes fully recovered, and she lowered her hand. She looked around, doing a full 360-degree turn. *I don't see them anywhere.*

"Hey assholes, this isn't funny," Kevin shouted from a distance.

Kate turned and spotted Kevin sitting up in the meadow grass no more than fifty feet away. She started walking toward him. "Hey!"

He looked over at Kate, squinted, and then raised his hand over his eyes. Kate knew he was having the same issues she'd had a few moments prior. Kevin stood quickly and stumbled a few times as he made his way over to Kate. "I'm serious, this isn't funny, where's my stuff?" His eyes nearly adjusted, he lowered his hand; as it went down, a red watch on his wrist caught his attention. "And what is this?"

"Not sure," Kate said as she met Kevin in the field. "I have one too." She raised her wrist for Kevin to observe.

Kevin looked back at his watch, turned his wrist over, and began to pick at the band with his finger.

"It's not coming off," Kate added. "I already tried; the band is seamless, and I couldn't get it to budge."

Shifting his attention back to Kate, Kevin dropped his arm to his side. "Chris better not have bolted with our gear..." Kevin began.

"No, I know him better than that. This is something else," she calmly interrupted. "The hills and mountains, they aren't right." Pointing at the surrounding terrain, Kate continued, "Sun is rising from over there, that means this is east. We should see the foothills we climbed two days ago right over there." Kate pointed straight ahead. "See? Flat, and then goes up sharply to the left. We're not anywhere near our camp."

"Then where the hell are we?"

The sun was rising quickly, and with it, the heat. Though their eyes had adjusted, the lack of cloud cover was rapidly hindering their ability to stay in the open. They both raised their hands above their eyes to block the sun. "We need to find some shade; we're going to get fried out here," Kate said as she gestured to Kevin to walk with her toward the closest tree line.

They walked a few hundred yards through the meadow toward the eastern tree line. Kevin stopped every few paces and continued to gaze in all directions for any signs of other campers or anything familiar. Kate kept her eyes on the tree line—she knew they were nowhere near the camp. She was growing increasingly sure they weren't even in the national park anymore.

"Hey guys!" Chris' voice reached from across the meadow. Kate and Kevin turned to see Chris making his way toward them. They held their position as he quickly trotted through the field, hopping over thick grass and dodging rocks.

"There you are," Chris said as he caught his breath. "You guys alright?"

"All things considered." Kevin shrugged.

"We're not in the park. This terrain is all wrong," Chris added as he looked around while catching his breath.

"Kate said the same thing; do you have any idea where we are?" Kevin added.

"No, none of this is familiar. And I woke up with this red wristwatch," Chris added as he raised his wrist, showing Kevin and Kate the red watch. "Pretty useless, can't get it to move off the number thirty-six. Not sure it's even built to tell time."

Kate stepped forward, looking at Chris' other hand. "Looks like that's not all you have." In his left hand, he was carrying a tin water bottle. The canteen easily fit in his palm, and a small black strap dangled from the lid.

"This?" Chris gestured to the bottle. "Yeah, it was attached to my belt when I woke up. Nothing in it though." He raised his hand and shook the canteen.

Kate paused and glared at the canteen, then abruptly swerved over and looked on Kevin. "Kevin, check your pockets," she added quickly as she drove her hands into her own.

Rummaging around, Kevin retrieved a folded red envelope from his back-left pocket.

Kate pulled a box of matches from the small cargo pocket near the bottom of her shorts.

"Interesting," Chris started. "What's in the envelope?" He pointed to Kevin.

Kevin looked down at the envelope in his hand. It was light and thin; the contents of the interior were minimal. The envelope was sealed with a wax stamp with the letters AP pressed into the center. "Any idea what this means?" Kevin held up the letter and exposed the seal to Kate and Chris.

Kate and Chris shook their heads.

Kevin looked down at the envelope, unbent it, carefully broke the wax seal, and extracted a piece of paper. Unfolding it, he glanced over it for a few moments, turning pale, he looked back up at Kate and Chris. "No way this is real," he said with dismissive anxiety.

"What does it say?" Chris inquired.

"See for yourself," Kevin said as he handed Chris the paper and sat down in the grass.

Kate walked over and joined Chris in reading the piece of paper.

Dear Christopher, Kathryn, and Kevin:

```
Congratulations! You've been selected to partake in a
real-world game of pursuit and conquest. Over the next
thirty-six hours, your exceptional problem-solving and
survival skills will be put to the test as you embark on a
journey that will undoubtedly bring you face-to-face with
dehydration, starvation, and mortal danger.

To get you started, your team has been provided with an
empty drinking canteen and box of matches. Use them wisely.

Those still standing at the end of thirty-six hours will be
declared winners and awarded a grand prize.

From all of us at APEX, we sincerely hope you enjoy the
pursuit.Thank you for your cooperation.
```

Kate looked up after reading the note and gazed over at Chris, who continued to stare at the page. Neither said a word. She was still trying to comprehend what she had just read twice and surmised Chris was in a similar situation.

Chris finally looked up, shook his head in disbelief, but remained very calm. "Well, that's one way to get our attention."

"Ever heard of APEX?" Kate asked as she pointed to the letter.

"Never," Chris replied. Though Chris knew this wasn't true. He distinctly remembered the Ranger fellow from a few days back mentioning APEX. He made the connection quickly and knew Ranger probably had something to with the letter and whatever was happening to them.

"I'm honestly more intrigued by the grand prize note at the bottom."

"Think we're on a game show or something?" Kevin added, still sitting in the brush.

"I doubt it. I never signed anything, and that would create a legal nightmare for these APEX folks," Kate added.

"Agree. Without a waiver, their liabilities would be through the roof,"

Chris agreed.

"Not to mention, we never gave consent to participate and be shipped out here." Kate paused. "Speaking of which, do either of you remember how we ended up out here? I got nothing."

Kevin shook his head.

Kate looked over at Chris, who was clearly contemplating his response. "I remember something strange about our last night at camp, but I can't put my finger on it. Last thing I truly remember was the thunder and leaving the tent to check our camp. Next thing, I'm sitting in this field and hearing you two talking in the distance."

There was a short pause. "Can we keep going toward the shade? It's getting salty out here," Kevin asked.

"Good idea. We should also probably get a sense for where we are." Chris stepped closer to Kate and pointed to the eastern hills. "I'm thinking we head up right there, should give us a good view of the terrain."

"Might also give us an idea of where we can find some water," Kate added.

"Exactly. When we find water, we follow it and hopefully pick up a trail or road or something that can get us back to civilization."

Chris and Kate helped Kevin to his feet and then walked toward the tree line, which quickly ascended and formed a mountainous hill that was several hundred feet high.

"Probably half a mile to the tree line, maybe another two to the top. We should be able to get there in just over an hour," Chris said as he headed toward the tree line. The crew marched swiftly toward the shade. Each knew getting out of the direct sun would immediately improve their situation. They had no idea how far away civilization or help could be, and the longer they spend in the direct sun, the greater risk of dehydration and sunburn.

Abruptly, Kevin stopped and looked to his left. "You guys hear that?"

Chris and Kate stopped, looking at Kevin as he remained focused on the horizon to his left.

Kate detected a soft flapping rumble in the distance. It was a constant sound and didn't appear to fade or get louder. "Is that a helicopter?"

"I think so," Kevin responded.

At that moment, a small object rose from the horizon and slowly moved away from their position. The sound quickly faded and disappeared in less than a minute. As the object faded into the horizon, all three red watches on their wrists vibrated simultaneously.

Kevin looked down at his wrist and observed the screen counting down from 36:00:00. "Well, whoever it was, they're gone now. And whatever this is, it has started," Kevin signed.

Kate looked up from her watch, and gazed anxiously over to Chris. "There's clearly something over there," she added while gesturing toward where the small object had disappeared from their line of sight.

"Right. If we can follow it, we might be able to get out of here today," Chris concluded as he pointed back at the hill they were previously pursuing.

Kate nodded at Chris, and they restarted the trek toward the tree line.

Kevin looked down at his watch again. 35:58:35. *Something is very wrong. That much is obvious. Do Kate and Chris not see this?* Though Kevin had spent sixty hours a week for the past few years solving complex coding challenges, the fundamental process of solving problems was very applicable to his current situation. It didn't take a rocket scientist to deduce they had been thrown into a foreign environment against their will. Gear needed for survival, gone. Food, gone. Water, gone. *Somebody carefully planned this. Somebody wanted to put us in this situation. But to what endgame? For what purpose? Or, are Kate and Chris hiding something from me?* Kate and Chris were already fifty feet ahead and pulling away. "Hey guys, wait up."

35:27:56

The tree line was predominately populated with tall Douglas firs and the occasional Western Hemlock, which Chris observed were more densely concentrated on the slope. Kate was first to reach the tree line, and Chris followed closely behind. While crossing the field, Kevin made up most of his ground, but still lagged by several paces. With the sun and temperature continuing to rise, Kate and Chris made no concerted effort to hold and wait for Kevin to catch up until they reached the shade.

"Need a minute?" Chris asked Kevin as he ducked into the shade and sat near Kate's feet.

"I'm good, just need a second," Kevin replied, panting, with streaks of sweat running down his face, which he wiped away with his forearm.

The ground was dry and patchy with tree roots and pine needles covering a majority of the terrain. Past the tree line, the incline was steeper than it looked from a distance. Chris knew this would be a challenge for the team and decided a short break made sense. He looked at Kate and gestured for her to kneel next to Kevin; he did the same. "Alright, I'm going to go ahead to see what the terrain looks like. Won't be more than a few minutes. That'll give you both a chance to cool down. Then we'll climb together."

Kate nodded. Kevin waved his hand while not making contact with either of them. He was clearly focused on cooling down.

Chris stood and quickly darted up the hill and out of view.

"Something isn't right about this," Kevin said to Kate.

"You already said that," she replied.

Kevin looked up at Kate. He was trying to evaluate the sincerity of the interaction. "Don't you find it strange that he didn't wake anywhere near us?"

"What do you mean?"

"I mean, you and I found each other around the same time, in similar proximity. We didn't spot Chris for several minutes, and when we did, he was in a completely different location."

"I guess," Kate replied, indicating she wanted him to continue.

"And I didn't even see where he came from, did you? He just appeared, yelling, waving, and running toward us." Kevin paused. "I don't know, something just feels off. And he even said he wasn't in his tent right before something happened."

Kate couldn't disagree with Kevin's points. "I hear you, and your points are well-taken. But he's stuck out here with us as well. He doesn't have his gear, and he's facing the same situation we are."

"Is he?"

Kate looked at him, wondering where he was going.

"We were literally paying him to teach us advanced camping skills—well, I am, at least. And we're now literally in a situation that's advantageous for exactly one of us."

"Speak for yourself." Kate sniffed.

"Okay, okay. You know that's not what I meant. But you see where I'm going, don't you? And where is he now? Conveniently up the hill and out of sight. Who knows what he's actually doing."

"I'm going to stop you there; he went up the hill because you needed a break, and time is critical. You should know this. We have no food, no water, and it's hot as hell out here. We needed to keep moving." Kate paused. "I know a lot of this doesn't make sense, and look, I agree

59

this situation is very suspicious, but right now, he's our best chance at getting out of this mess. I think we need to cut him some slack."

Kevin realized he'd gotten Kate thinking about his concerns, but she was also right about Chris; he was clearly their best bet to get home—*even if he has a hand in why we're here.* Kevin looked up at Kate and nodded. "You're right." He pushed himself up and dusted off his clothes and legs. "We need to keep moving."

As Kate stood to join Kevin, a series of soft thumps and cracking branches approached their location. Seconds later, Chris emerged into their line of sight. He was trotting down the hill, making short strides and keeping his eyes on the ground so as not to trip. He made his way over to Kate and Kevin.

"Terrain isn't too bad," he began while catching his breath. "Steep in a few areas, but the footing looks okay. It'll take longer than I originally thought, but we can probably get to the top in a few hours. Not sure if it opens up across the top, but if anything, we'll be at a better vantage point to figure out where we are." Chris paused to see if Kate or Kevin had any questions. Both remained silent. "I'll go first and make sure our path is safe."

Kevin looked over at Kate, and then to Chris. "Lead the way."

***

The trek up the hill was a slow grind. As Chris had described, the incline was predictable, except in a few spots where they had to climb over downed trees and the occasional boulder protruding from the hillside. The tree cover was mostly ubiquitous and provided much-needed shade for the crew to continue their hike.

Kate's calves began to burn with each step and further shifted her focus downward. It was several moments later that Chris stopped ahead. In his hand, he held a branch vertically. Using his free hand, Chris stripped small growths and debris from the main branch and used a nearby stone to smooth the surface. Kate approached him and paused.

"Not the hiking poles you're used to, but I promise this will help." He handed her the branch and began to work on another. "Watch out for slivers. Smoothed out a few spots there in the middle for your hands. Wood looks good; it should be able to bear weight and not snap in your hands."

"Thanks," Kate said as she accepted the branch and inspected the spots Chris had called out.

Kevin arrived shortly after Kate and looked over at Chris' work.

"Don't worry, I'm making one for you right now." Chris smirked while looking at Kevin.

"Good call," Kevin responded.

A few short minutes later, Chris had the second branch ready, in Kevin's hands, and they continued up the hill.

The crew scaled the hill for another hour, with each step more grueling than the last. They struggled up the incline with Chris in front, roughly ten paces ahead of Kate. Similar to every point thus far, Kevin trailed behind Kate, but only by a few paces. Kate was intentionally holding close to Kevin in the event he needed some assistance. She recalled a trip a few summers back where their group had attempted a similar climb, nothing out of the ordinary, but one of the new campers wasn't physically prepared for the climb, grew weak, lost his balance, and rolled his ankle during his fall. Kate believed that, had somebody paid closer attention, they might have picked up signs he was in trouble and could have mitigated the injury. Instead, the weekend ended abruptly. Remaining mindful of Kevin's demeanor and breathing, Kate slowed her pace.

The hill began to slowly flatten near the peak, and with it came several changes to the terrain as the trees thinned and the ground became more congested with protruding boulders and rocky surfaces. This slowed their march as footing became increasingly treacherous and they took caution as they continued forward with heads down and shortened strides. Chris, now even farther ahead, occasionally shouted back to Kate and Kevin with a "heads up" or remarks on an upcoming step. Kevin appreciated the warnings as he found their new terrain comparable to navigating a minefield.

"Think there are snakes up here?" Kevin asked Kate as they marched forward.

"Beyond a doubt. Watch your step," Kate said sarcastically as she looked back at Kevin and smiled.

Returning her attention forward, Kate abruptly stopped. Up ahead, Chris stood motionless as he peered forward. The tree cover around him mostly dissipated. The terrain was almost completely compromised of stone and small growths that sprouted between the cracks. Kate glanced back toward Kevin.

"Think we're at the top?" he asked.

"I think so."

"Thank God. I need a rest."

"Stay here for a second," Kate said as she gestured for him to take a seat while she investigated.

As Kate approached, Chris moved forward. Within a few steps he disappeared from her line of sight. A soft clashing rumble emerged as she drew closer to where Chris had previously stood. Arriving where Chris previously stood, Kate quickly realized why he had stopped. The terrain ahead started to slope downward, and then abruptly ended. At the point where land was no longer visible, all she could see was a sea of blue. Scanning her forward periphery, Kate quickly realized they were surrounded by water, a lot of water, with no land in sight. Peering down the slope, she saw Chris, some fifty feet ahead, sitting down on the rocky terrain, staring off into the distance. She began her descent toward him.

Noticing Kate had now disappeared from view, Kevin decided to make his way up the stone terrain. *I need to stop letting these guys take off on me.* He picked up his pace toward where he had last seen Kate and Chris. Cresting the hill, Kevin looked down the decline and found them sitting together on the ground, gazing out at the blue horizon. Looking up, he squinted and shifted his focus to the horizon. His eyes quickly grew large as he realized what he was seeing. *Shit.*

33:37:04

Keeping his left foot in front and right foot turned square behind his center of gravity, Chris slowly inched forward. Several minutes had passed since he'd decided somebody had to take a look. From a distance, he thought the task should be simple, but as he inched closer to the edge, the wind gusts became stronger, and the crashing waves below grew louder. *This is probably close enough.* He squatted down on the stone ledge, shifted to his knees, and carefully rolled forward using his elbows. He peered over the edge; it was as bad as he'd feared.

Moments later, Chris returned to Kate and Kevin, who hadn't moved from their seated positions. Looking down at his watch, Chris shook his head as he realized it had only been fourteen minutes since he'd reached the top, and his trip to the cliff took fewer than five. *Felt like I was gone for at least a half-hour.*

"What's the word?" Kevin asked as he looked up at Chris.

"Sharp decline, at least a thousand feet, probably closer to fifteen hundred." He ran his fingers through his hair. "Even if we managed to get down there, the surf would make quick work of us. I didn't see anywhere safe to walk."

"And it was like that everywhere?" asked Kate.

"From what I could see. At least along this ridge." Chris put his hands on his hips and looked back toward the trees where they'd recently hiked. "I think this is an island; that would also explain why we can't see anything after the hills on the other side." Chris pointed to the mountainous hills to the west that rose over the tree line.

"So, what do we do next?" Kevin asked.

"Still think heading north is the best bet; the terrain opens up down there," Chris replied as he shifted his gaze north.

"Toward where we heard that helicopter?" Kate asked.

"Yeah, our plan hasn't really changed. But I do think we need to find water, and fast."

"How do you propose we do that?" added Kevin.

"We need to resurvey where we are first. Best course of action is to head back to the tree line and climb up and take a look."

"You mean climb to the top of one of those?" Kevin asked while pointing. "Some of those are pushing sixty, seventy feet tall."

"I know. If I can find one with lower branches, the climb shouldn't be..."

"We both know I'm the better climber." Kate interrupted as she stood. "Chris is right, we need to reorient ourselves. I'll do it."

Chris nodded at Kate, who walked over and offered her hand to Kevin. Continuing to fix his gaze on the horizon, Kevin didn't immediately take her hand. "Or we can sit here," she added. Kevin glared up at Kate, shook his head, and apprehensively took her hand.

Making their way back to the tree line, the crew began to evaluate climbing options. "What are you looking for?" Kevin asked.

"Prefer something with lower branches; my shoes have good grip, but pulling myself up is always easier than scaling," she replied while evaluating a group of trees on the edge of the hill. The majority of trees on this end of the forest were Western Hemlock, and the lowest branches were several feet out of reach, and those that had surface area weeping down within reach weren't capable of supporting any meaningful weight. They needed to find a sturdy branch right at the trunk of a tree.

Shifting course, they made their way north along the tree line. Kevin and Kate inspected trees within a few paces of the break, and Chris explored inward, slightly downslope where the trees grew larger. "What about this one?" Chris shouted up to Kate as he pointed up at a large tree with branches starting at the trunk around a foot or two above his head. "I can boost you up," he added. Kate looked down at Chris, gave him a thumbs-up, and then gestured for Kevin to follow her down the hill toward Chris.

Kate looked up from the base of the tree and walked a full circle around. "Looks okay to me, but yeah, I'll need a boost up to that first branch," she began. Walking over to the left side of the trunk, she gestured toward the lowest branch, which appeared several inches thick. "I'm thinking right here." Chris joined her and looked up, nodding in agreement.

"Step back for a second," Chris said as he approached the tree and put the trunk right behind his left shoulder. Chris spread his legs and set a firm stance. Looking down, he interlocked his fingers and flexed and stretched in his stance. Releasing his hands, he looked over to Kate and nodded.

She approached and stood in front of him. "Good to go?" she began.

"Yes. Put your left foot right here," he began as he relocked his hands together, "and use the tree for balance as you go for the branch."

"Got it," Kate said as she put her left foot into his hands while leaving her right on the ground. "Ready?"

"Yup, ready when you are."

Kate nodded, kicked off with her right foot, and shifted her weight onto the leg in Chris' hands. In one motion, she pushed up, he slowly lifted, and she reached high into the air toward the branch. Stretching mightily and knowing time was critical, Kate shouted down to Chris, "Need a few more inches, almost there."

Taking a deep breath, Chris raised his arms higher and sent Kate another foot into the air. Above, he heard the shaking of a branch, and a second later, her foot left his hands and she was gone. Clutching the branch with both hands, Kate wasted little time and swung one leg over.

Peering into the growth, Kate grabbed a second branch above and quickly found her balance. Pausing slightly, she shifted her weight and continued the ascent. With a swing and a push, Kate rose another level. As she ascended, the branches came closer together, which made the ascent similar to climbing a ladder. The branches smacked her as she bent and pulled her way higher. She was slowed for a moment by a spider web in her climbing path that ended up in her face. Wiping it clear, she quickly continued her ascent.

Watching Kate from below, Chris and Kevin stood in awe at how quickly she ascended the tree. "She just climbed like fifty feet in a few minutes," Kevin said, not taking his eyes off of her.

"She needs to get another ten to twenty up," Chris added quietly. "Close to the canopy so she can actually see something. That's also where the tree is the least stable."

Kevin paused, not taking his eyes off of Kate's general location, and shifted the conversation. "So, you really don't have any idea what's going on?"

Chris looked over at Kevin. "What do you mean?"

Kevin turned his head and met Chris' eyes. "A lot of this doesn't add up. I find it hard to believe none of us has a clue why we're here."

"Why do you think we're here?"

"That's that part I haven't put together yet," Kevin replied as he looked back up toward Kate. "But I'm pretty sure one of us knows something they're not telling the others."

Chris continued to look at Kevin. It was clear he was very suspicious, likely of him. This wasn't a constructive turn of events; Chris knew they needed to keep calm and work together if they were going to get out.

"I can assure you, I had nothing to do with this, if that's what you're implying," Chris began. Kevin broke his gaze and looked back at Chris. "That being said, do you remember that man we met on the trail?"

"The guy with the safari hat? Yeah," Kevin replied, "What was his name again?"

"Ranger. And while we were alone, before you and Kate came over that first morning, he and I made small talk."

Kevin nodded for Chris to continue.

"He mentioned working for a company called APEX."

"From that red letter? Do you think it's the same one?"

"Yes, I do. The coincidence is too on-point. He has something to do with all of this, I just don't know what."

"Did he tell you anything about APEX?"

"Only that they specialized in some sort of entertainment." Chris shrugged.

Kevin paused, still looking at him. *I think he's probably telling the truth.* "Does Kate know about any of this?"

"Nope. I didn't want to spook either of you until I was sure."

"And you're sure now?"

"Not at all. But I need us to trust each other. This situation is far more dangerous than you think. In this weather, we could easily dehydrate out here, or take a nasty spill on these rocks. If one of us goes down, we will need to work together."

"Think one of us is going down at some point?"

"Not if I can help it," Chris replied as he looked back up at Kate.

Far above, Kate continued her ascent. Birds flapped from nearby trees as the branches swayed and smacked each other with each climbing step. The warmth of the sun on her shoulders was becoming more prominent as well. *Must be getting close; the trees aren't shielding me anymore.* Up above, the tree coverage quickly broke and opened up into blue sky. Taking a few more cautious steps, she broke through.

Adjusting her grip, she looked up at the tree and then back to the trunk and elected to stop climbing. The branches had become increasingly smaller, as had the trunk. A few more feet up and she wasn't sure if the newer growth could support her weight.

Kate shifted her position and looked down from her perch at the sea of trees on the hill below. The incline provided sufficient height separation between trees for her to view the terrain beyond. Down and to her left, the meadow where the day's events began came into view. Farther to the northwest, she made out another series of large mountainous hills. Peering back at the landscape below, she drew her eyes right toward the northern tree line of the meadow. A thick forest of trees made up the entire landscape. However, it opened back up after a few miles. Squinting, she looked deeper into the opening. She smiled at what she saw along the tree line. *Bingo.*

Several minutes later, Kate was back on the ground with Kevin and Chris. Dusting herself off, she began to explain what she'd seen: hills to the west, and the forest to the north.

"After the tree line, it opens up again. Not sure how large the field is, but along the edge, I definitely saw a shimmer," she elaborated.

"What does a shimmer mean? People?" Kevin inquired.

"A shimmer means the sun is refracting off of something," Chris added.

"Right, and the shimmer popped up in a few spots along the tree line; my guess is it's a river," Kate concluded.

"So, we're heading there next?" Kevin asked as he looked down the hillside.

Chris turned and looked north. "No, we should stay up here. If there's a river, it's being fed from somewhere, likely in these hills. If that's the case, we'll find a spring or stream up ahead."

"And then we make our way down where everything converges?" Kate confirmed.

"Probably. Was the shimmer in the same direction as the helicopter?" Chris asked.

Kate nodded. "Same relative direction."

"Okay, yeah. Let's keep the high ground. We can head this way," Chris said as he pointed north. "Let's find some water, and then make our way down where the streams converge. Then we can make our way north through the field Kate saw, and that should get us more or less in line with where we saw the helicopter. Cool?"

"Agreed," Kevin said. Kate nodded in agreement.

The crew turned and started heading north along the cresting hilltops.

32:15:07

K evin's parents had migrated to the United States in the mid-eighties. His father, an orphan, dedicated his entire life to the betterment of his family. Never once had Kevin heard his father complain or acknowledge he was having a bad day. Though his father's life was never short of challenges, Kevin slowly found his father led a life of relentless struggle. Keven never truly understood his father. Even as a young man, he found himself contemplating how someone could grow from the depths of an orphan upbringing, through an arduous blue-collar adulthood, bringing his family across the ocean, to seeing his one and only child graduate with honors from Berkeley.

A life of unexpected challenges, poorly dealt hands, and yet his father had found the genuine strength to carry on and find a purpose that would impact future generations of his family in ways he'd never imagine. This always stuck with Kevin. The notion of living up to the impact his father made, as he perceived it, was why he went into innovation, and also why he spent his summers methodically attempting new skills. *Why the hell did I think taking up camping was a good idea?*

The sun was nearing the midday sky. Rays of sunshine pierced the sparse canopy and lit up the forest floor. Cloud cover remained sparse, and the heat of the sun on their shoulders was growing increasingly intense. Luckily, the wind had picked up a little, giving the crew a small breeze as they continued their route north. Their progress was slow and methodical. Though they were no longer hiking an incline, the terrain at the top of the hill remained mostly protruding rocks and boulders.

Kate wasn't entirely sure how far they had gone—at least two miles, and still no viable water source. There was one instance where Kevin spotted a muddy puddle at the base of a tree's root system, but they decided to push on after finding an assortment of green and brown debris in the water.

"Keep your eyes peeled," Chris began. "What we're looking for could be very small."

"What exactly are we looking for again?" Kevin asked.

"A natural water spring or some sort of stream," Chris replied. "The spring, in particular, might be tough to spot if there isn't any pooling, so just let us know if you see any places where the ground looks particularly damp."

Kevin stopped looking down the slope to his left. "You mean like right there?" Kevin pointed down the hill from his feet at a dark spot on the ground, mostly covered in needles and assorted forest debris, but clearly wet. Chris and Kate stopped abruptly and pivoted toward where Kevin was pointing.

Wasting little time, Chris darted down the hill and evaluated the wet spot. He got on his knees and began to clear away the surrounding area. With the debris removed, he began to claw small holes in the ground. As he dug, a damp roll of water flowed past his knees.

Kevin came down to see. "What do you think?"

"I think you just found us a tiny spring. It's not huge and was getting spread by everything on the floor, but if you see here, we clearly have a steady stream coming out."

"Found another over here," Kate said from a few meters downhill. "Looks like we might have a few small sources in this area, and I think they're converging down there." Kate pointed downhill.

Chris waved Kate over to where he and Kevin were standing. She walked in their direction. Carefully, Chris took out the water canteen, pressed it to the ground, and let the small trickle of water flow in.

"Is that safe to drink?" Kevin asked.

"Should be fine," Chris replied while keeping his focus on the canteen. "This is a natural spring, it's as good as we're going to do out here." After a few moments, Chris withdrew the canteen from the ground, raised it to his nose, took a quick sniff, and then took a swig. The elation in his face was obvious to Kevin and Kate. Chris took a second gulp, smiled, and handed the canteen to Kevin.

Chris turned to Kate. "They converge down there, you said?" He gestured down the hill where she once stood.

"Yea. Only a few inches wide, but a clear directional flow."

"Good. Once we're done here, let's follow it. I know we've only gone a few miles so far, but if we were to descend the hill, we should at least land pretty close to the far tree line, no?"

"I'm not sure, if I'm being honest," Kate replied. "There was clearly a break in the tree line, but I couldn't tell you if it was two or four miles."

"But close enough to make the descent? I don't want to give up high ground just to meander down and end up near the meadow again."

"Oh no, we're well into the forest. It's just a question of how much farther we'll have at the bottom."

Kevin walked up to Chris and handed him the empty canteen. Chris placed the container back at the mouth of the spring and began to refill. "Works for me; let's follow and see where we end up. I have a feeling we're going to find that river before too long," Chris added as he looked back up at Kate.

The crew enjoyed a few more rounds of fluid; Kate was the recipient of the next refresh. After a short rest, Chris refilled, hooked the canteen to his belt, and began his way toward the trickle Kate found.

***

The trickle carried along laterally across the hillside at a slight downward angle. Over the previous thirty minutes, the crew had observed the trickle more than double in width and perceived depth. They stopped a few times to replenish their water supply, as Kevin found it apt to empty the entire canteen over his head, more than once.

"This thing is starting to pick up," Kate said to Chris as he bent over the trickle and filled the canteen.

"For sure. We have a lot of moisture up here. It has to go somewhere."

"How much farther, do you think?"

"By me, I'm thinking we keep following as long as this thing keeps growing. If we hit a dead end, we reassess," Chris concluded as he stood and fastened the canteen to his side.

For the first time all trip, they continued on with Kevin in the lead.

"Just follow the water." Chris gestured to Kevin as he and Kate followed.

As they progressed downhill, the rocky terrain began to dissipate and return to hard dirt and tree root systems. Chris was confident they hadn't given up more than a third of their morning's climb, but he was reluctant to descend farther without a meaningful source of water.

Slowing his march, Kevin paused and turned his head left. Kate and Chris caught up and met with him.

"What is it?" Kate asked.

Kevin smiled. "You hear that?"

They all listened intently. In the distance, they could make out a soft rush. Chris smiled as well. "That, my friends, is water, and a lot more than what we're following right now." Chris pushed forward and began walking toward the sound. Kate and Kevin quickly followed behind. "I knew these had to converge somewhere," he added.

The crew briskly made their way through the trees, not losing sight of the trickle they had been following. The sun continued to shine down through the trees. Kate could tell the sun was past midday, and they were approaching early afternoon. The rushing sound grew louder. They were getting close.

In a short burst, Chris turned back to Kate and Kevin, waved for them to follow, and took off running. They both accelerated and continued to follow him. Moments later, all three broke through and were standing at the edge of a small river. The current, moderately strong, swept along the hillside down toward the valley below. The river was roughly fifteen feet across and didn't appear impassable. Chris hesitated for only a second and then stepped in. Moments later, he was wading in water up to his waist. He smiled, and then, in one motion, dunked himself under and sprang back up through the surface. "Ahh!" he shouted.

"How is it?" Kevin asked.

"Very cold," Chris replied as he made his way back to the river's edge. "Current isn't too bad, though. And I don't think it gets much deeper. We can definitely cross if we need to."

Before Chris could arrive at the bank, Kate and Kevin stepped into the river and waded toward Chris. Kate, clearly freezing, smiled in elation as she sunk into the water. Kevin entered with more caution, taking small steps and keeping his upper body and head well above the waterline. He made his way over as if he were tiptoeing through the river.

"Move on or take a break?" Kevin asked the others.

"Let's cool down for a few more minutes, and then, honestly, I think we follow this down," Chris began. "Even if there's nothing in the valley, we'll at least have a steady water source, and if we follow it long enough, we'll eventually find somebody or something that can help us."

"Uhh. I'm hungry." Kate groaned as she stood up. The water was waist-high on her.

75

"Yeah, me too. I don't think there will be much in this river," Chris added as he looked uphill at the river. "There might be something in the valley, but odds are we'll need to get creative."

Kevin returned to the shore, leaving Kate and Chris to their menu scheming, and surveyed the surrounding terrain on both sides of the river. There were tight and dense trees on both sides. The river flow was steady, but he agreed with Chris' assessment that crossing shouldn't be an issue, at least from their current vantage point. He wasn't able to see the top of the hill anymore; it quickly disappeared into the tree line above. Kevin found the smell especially refreshing, the mist of the river joining the aroma of pine. The aroma combined with the steady sound of the flowing river brought him a sense of ease for the first time all day. Inhaling deeply, Kevin abruptly paused and smelled hard again with suspicion. *Smoke.*

"Hey guys!" Kevin shouted as he interrupted Chris and Kate's meal planning.

"What's up?" Kate replied as she turned around.

"You smell that?"

"Smell what?" Chris asked.

"Smoke. It's very distinct over here."

Chris looked at Kate, and in one motion they both quickly made their way to the shore where Kevin stood.

"I'm not smelling anything," Kate said.

"Stand right here," Kevin said as he gestured for them to come back on land and walk a few steps from the edge. They both did as he asked and inhaled deeply.

After a short pause, Chris looked at Kate. "He's right. It's faint, but definitely smoke."

"Where's it coming from?" Kate asked.

Chris bent over and ripped a few pieces of grass he found at the base of a tree. Peering at the tree line on the other side of the river, he tossed the pieces of grass in the air. They quickly floated behind him and landed behind his right shoulder. "Alright, we're downwind. If I had to guess, it's probably coming from over there," he said, pointing across the river and slightly back up the hill.

"What's our next move?" Kevin asked Chris.

"We need to go investigate. Maybe it's somebody who can help us."

"Or, it's the person who put us out here," Kevin muttered.

There was a long pause. The crew was clearly contemplating Kevin's remark, which, under the circumstances, made a lot of sense.

"Either way, we need to see what's going on. Let's just approach cautiously. I'll go first," Chris concluded.

One by one, Chris, Kate, and Kevin entered the river and waded across to the other side. Chris' evaluation of the river held up; the water line never came within six inches of his shoulders, and the current, though stronger in the middle, was very manageable as long as they watched their steps. The biggest challenge of the crossing was finding a good place to make shore. The shoreline was mostly composed of muddy, densely rooted overhang, but Chris managed to find a spot where they could use a stone and an overhanging branch to easily emerge from the river. Moments later, all three were on the opposite shore.

31:25:11

Taking a quick survey of their position, Chris led the crew into the woods. The smell of smoke was becoming increasingly prevalent. He had a good idea of where to head and kept the crew downwind of the smoke. During their ascent, he paused a few times and motioned to Kate and Kevin, who were hanging back, to get down. He would peer around the woods, resume a standing position, and then motion for them to follow.

Continuing the climb, Chris paused abruptly, leaned against a nearby tree as he stood on his tiptoes, peered for a few seconds uphill, and then crouched down and backtracked to Kevin and Kate. "Alright, there's definitely something just up on the ridge. Maybe a hundred feet. You two stay here, I'm going to take a look," Chris said.

Kevin and Kate nodded as Chris turned around and quietly darted up the hill.

Landing softly with each step and doing his best to avoid stepping on twigs or anything that would potentially give away his position, he quickly made his way up the hill. Moments later, the target came into view. In front of him, a small plume of smoke rose into the canopy.

Chris slowed his pace and evaluated his surroundings. He needed a safe way to get closer without compromising his position. Slowly moving between the trees, avoiding nearby brush and loose gravel, Chris made his way toward the smoke. Having a closer look, the smoke was coming from a small ledge on the hillside. *That's where I'd want to camp.*

Sneaking up to the right ledge, leaving the river to his far right and smoke to his left, Chris found a large tree to set position and scope the situation. Carefully peering around the trunk, Chris quickly observed a small man-made fire cracking a few paces from the tree; the burning logs were neatly positioned in a triangular configuration. Close to the flames, Chris spotted a small pack of food sitting upright next to a backpack nestled in the nearby brush. *Where are you?*

Chris waited quietly behind the tree for any sign of movement. The wind softly rustled the treetops as Chris held his breath, alert to his surroundings. Moments later a man emerged from beyond the fire. He was tightening his shorts, having clearly stepped away to relieve himself. Chris got a good look at the man; they were similar in age, and he was not particularly tall or fit but was sporting some pretty impressive camping attire, including a knife sleeve on his belt line. Leaning in, Chris could make out a white device on the man's wrist. It wasn't the same as the red one on Chris's wrist, but there were definite similarities in design.

The man walked up to the fire and reached down to a pot nestled on the far side of the fire and brought it toward the open pouch on the ground. Pouring the contents into the pot, he turned back to the fire, paused for a moment as if he were evaluating what to do next, and then set the entire meal into the heart of the flames. In a retracting motion from burning his hand, the man dropped it upright into the fire. *This guy seems pretty harmless. I'd be more afraid of Kevin.* Chris smirked and debated his next move.

The man quietly cursed to himself as he lifted a black bow from the brush and swiped its end into the flames, trying to salvage his meal. Evaluating the situation, Chris determined this was the time to make his presence known. *The man is out of his element; maybe I can offer assistance as my in.* Chris rounded the tree and slowly walked toward the cracking fire. Taking soft steps toward the man, whose gaze was still upon the pot, Chris quickened his pace slightly. With a soft crunch, he stepped on dry debris along his route and prematurely gave away his position. Chris froze as the man's gaze darted up and looked around. Moments later, he was making eye contact with Chris. Neither man moved nor said a word.

Taking a step forward, Chris decided to break the standoff. "Need a hand with that?"

The man remained motionless. He was clearly taken aback. Clenching his bow across his chest with both hands and standing erect, he slowly took a few steps backward, away from the flames. Not once taking his eyes off of Chris.

"Sorry if I surprised you. Was hiking nearby, I smelled the smoke." Chris cautiously continued, "You need a hand with that?"   Chris gestured toward the pot.

The man remained still and unresponsive, until suddenly, and to Chris' surprise, he knelt down into his camping gear along the brush and withdrew an arrow. In a relatively quick motion, he notched the arrow, aimed it at Chris, and fired. The arrow screamed over the fire and whipped past Chris, over his left shoulder. The man quietly cursed to himself and reached back down to his gear.

Returning his gaze up with a second arrow, the man stood and began to walk toward the tree line. Chris had already taken off. He knew something about the man was off, and the second he saw the arrow and draw, he had turned and begun to dart down the hill. He zig-zagged down the slope as fast as the terrain would allow. Tree roots and rocks slowed his descent, but he was still going fast enough where one wrong step would likely result in an ugly tumble.

Without looking back, Chris ran toward Kate and Kevin, who glanced up at him, immediately realizing that something was wrong. "Go, go, go!" Chris shouted as he grabbed them both by the shoulders and pushed them to drop everything and run.

Kevin hesitated slightly as he stood up. "What is it?" he shouted to Chris as he continued to run down the slope. Looking back up the hill, Kevin caught the breeze of an object flying his direction. In a single motion, he dipped his upper body back just in time to see an arrow rip past his torso and into the ground. Completely taken aback, and not entirely sure of what just happened, he looked back up the hill and caught the shadow of an individual making his way down the hill in his direction. Not wasting another second, Kevin turned and darted down the slope toward Chris and Kate, who were already several paces ahead.

Rounding trees and dodging larger stones, Chris tried to slow his pace as his rate of descent was slowly getting away from him. Kate easily kept pace and remained close. There was no sign of Kevin, but Chris assumed he was close as well, though he didn't dare risk slowing down to confirm; he needed to keep his eyes on the terrain.

Continuing down the hill, Chris began to evaluate his periphery. *We can't keep running. We need to find a place to hide.* Peering over his left toward the river, he spotted a group of small trees and brush growth at the base of some dense pines. He adjusted course and made his way left. Kate followed, and Kevin shortly thereafter, who had closed the gap and arrived only a few steps later.

Sliding to a stop, Chris pivoted to a crouch and looked back up the hill. Kate and Kevin were right on him. He gestured for them to go into the brush and held a finger to his mouth. They both nodded as they arrived and slid down behind him. Looking up at the hill, Chris couldn't see or hear anything. The assailant was nowhere to be found. *He's up there somewhere.*

Slowly backing out of sight and into the brush, Chris turned to Kate and Kevin, who were sitting behind the cover, panting and trying to understand what was happening.

"What the hell was that about?" Kevin whispered to the crew.

Chris looked at Kevin and gestured. *Be quiet.*

"What's going on?" Kate whispered while looking between Kevin and Chris.

"We have a problem," Chris replied as he peered around the corner.

"I don't know about you, but I almost got kabobbed by someone up on the hill," Kevin whispered back, still catching his breath.

Kate paused and looked at Kevin as his hands trembled. She shifted her gaze over to Chris. "We're not alone?"

Chris shifted and brought his attention back to Kate and Kevin. "That's right, and he's not friendly," Chris added, "and we need to improve our position. I only have one vantage point from here."

"How many were there? Just one?" Kate asked.

"I think so," Chris replied. Pausing for a moment, he gestured for Kate to take his position, and he pointed to the north side of the brush and then back to himself. *You take up post here, I'll go up there for a better view.*

Crunch. Crunch. Snap.

Chris immediately lowered his head and gestured to Kate and Kevin for complete silence. The sound of footsteps grew louder. The steps didn't appear to be in any hurry. *He's looking for us, and he knows we're close.*

Looking over at Kate, Chris gestured for her to peer around the brush and see if she could spot the approaching individual. "Be careful," he mouthed to her.

Inching forward, Kate peered around the brush. Nothing caught her eye at first, and then in one split motion, a man emerged into her line of sight. He was some fifty feet away and not looking in her direction. Young and sporting some impressive gear, the man walked with a bow and arrow in hand and a backpack over his right shoulder. She could clearly make out a white device on the man's wrist.

The man paused and began to look around. Kate withdrew her head a few inches to minimize the odds of being spotted. Shifting his gaze to the ground, the man lightly kicked some rocks and dirt with his left foot in bored frustration and continued down the hill. Kate watched him for several paces as he disappeared from her sight.

Leaning back around the brush, Kate glanced over at Chris and Kevin, who were intently looking at her for an update. "One person," she gestured with her hand. "Going down the hill that way," she mouthed, pointing down the hill and slightly to the north.

Chris nodded and paused for a moment. *We should stick close to the water, but it's also probably no coincidence that we spotted this person near water as well. If Kate's correct, he was heading downhill, so perhaps heading uphill makes sense, but that march is slower, and the water supply might dwindle. There's also a cliff at the top, so if we're pursued, there's nowhere to go. We now have the high ground on him; following him could be our way out of here, but it would be risky. He's armed, and we're not. One thing is clear, if we stay here, we're not getting out.* Chris looked up to Kevin and Kate with a plan.

"I think we should go after this guy," Kevin whispered.

"Are you crazy?" replied Kate.

"Think about it. There's three of us, and one of him. Yes, he has a bow, but reloading after shots takes time. We could set up a kill box and corner him," Kevin concluded.

"I've seen him up close," Chris interrupted. "He's not a bad shot; it was only luck that he missed me up top. I think if we go after him, we could probably take him, but there's a good chance he'd clip one of us in the process. I don't think that's a risk we can take right now." Chris paused and continued, "But Kevin is right. We need to get out of here, and we need to keep tabs on this guy. It won't be easy, but we should track him from a distance. We can keep close to water, as long as he does, and maybe, just maybe, he could be our ticket out of here."

"I don't know about this," Kate replied. "He's heading downhill and has cut off our path to the valley or whatever is below. What if we head back to the top of the hill and reassess our position and strategy?"

"Not enough time. We can't spend the afternoon rescaling these hills," Chris replied, looking up at the sky. "Plus, if this guy doubles back, then we're pinned between him and a cliff. At least down there the terrain is more open, and I like our chances on a level playing field."

Hesitant, Kate looked over at Kevin, who was nodding toward Chris. Two against one, and they needed to stick together. Kate looked back and reluctantly nodded in agreement with Chris.

Slowing standing, Chris made his way around the brush, followed closely by Kate, then Kevin. Chris, keeping his head down and voice low, gestured back to Kate. "Where did you see him?"

Kate pointed forward as they continued to walk out away from the cover. Slowly making their way between trees along the hillside, Kate guided them to where she'd seen the man with the white watch. Several paces later they halted over scuff marks on the ground. Kate pointed into the dirt. Chris understood this to be the spot where the trail started, if there was one.

Looking around for a few moments, Chris spotted what he was looking for: a faint disturbance in the dirt from a boot. He remembered the man's attire from back up on the hill. *Those boots were very high quality; the treads are going to leave a mark on impact.* Gesturing Kate and Kevin over, Chris showed them the footprint and motioned for them to follow as he proceeded slowly down the hill.

The trail was faint at times, but Chris managed to follow the pair of tracks for at least one hundred paces. Pausing every so often to resurvey the land and listen for any noises, Chris led their descent. He continued to keep his head low, his steps short, and went out of his way to avoid unnecessary sounds. Kate and Kevin did as well.

Moments later, Chris paused by a large tree and gestured for Kate and

Kevin to join him. "How fast was this guy walking?" he whispered to Kate.

"Not fast at all. I'm surprised we haven't caught him yet," she replied.

"Me too. Not even a sign of him." *And he wasn't exactly keeping things quiet.*

Whoosh!

In a split second, an arrow ripped through the crew and struck Chris in the shoulder. All three ducked in reaction and pivoted around the large tree. Kate looked over at Chris. There was no arrow, but he was holding his arm, with blood dripping down to his elbow and on to the ground. "I'm alright, clipped my shoulder," Chris mouthed to Kate and Kevin as he grimaced.

The arrow came from uphill. How did he get position on us? Chris looked at the dirt and closed his eyes in frustration. A fake trail. This guy isn't nearly as incompetent as I thought. We shouldn't stay here. "We need to go now," Chris mouthed to Kevin and Kate, who both agreed.

In a single motion, all three pushed off from the tree and ran down the hill.

A second arrow whipped over Kate's shoulder, missing her by several inches, and clunked into a nearby tree.

The crew made their way down the hill. Kate made lunging strides as she passed Chris, who was still holding his bloody shoulder. Looking over at Kate, he pointed with his free hand to their left. "The river," he blurted mid-stride.

They continued to race downhill and through the thicket, and nobody paused to look back. The arrows had ceased, but there was zero doubt amongst the crew that they were still being pursued. In the distance, a loud rumble of the river rose. Over boulders, around trees, they didn't let up pace as they pushed farther. They were now in a full-on sprint down the hillside, occasionally glancing at each other to make sure they stayed together. The rumble of the river grew louder.

That sounds a lot louder than before. Where are we going? Chris thought to himself as he attempted to keep pace with Kate.

Seconds later, the terrain quickly became solid stone, and the trees thinned. "Whoa," Kate said as she spread both arms out, motioning to Kevin and Chris to stop. They had reached the river, but the crossing wasn't as expected. Now more than thirty feet wide, the river current was significantly stronger.

"We can't cross this," Kevin said, panting. "We need to continue down the hill."

Kate trotted quickly across the stone to the edge of the river and peered down. The water rushed past her gaze as a soft mist rose from the river. The rumble was loud and continuous. Staring for a moment and shaking her head, she turned around and trotted back to Kevin and Chris.

"It's a waterfall, at least fifty feet down, then it looks like it smooths out quite a bit. I think we're near the bottom," she said, looking at Kevin and Chris. Gazing beyond their stance, she caught a flicker from the tree line between their heads. Peering closely, she made out the silhouette of a person. He was crouched against a tree as the sun reflected from the surface of his watch. Bow drawn, he stayed motionless with a grin on his face.

"Shit, go!" Kate yelled as she ducked, pivoted, and ran toward the ledge. Kevin and Chris quickly followed. Not wasting another second, and without hesitation, they lunged off the stone edge and into the mist.

30:47:02

M r. White stood in amazement along the riverbank. Catching his breath, he bent over and wiped debris from his shin. With his pack around his shoulder and bow in hand, his forearm continued to tremble from the shots he had fired. The adrenaline rush was unlike anything he had felt before, and the recent events were very unexpected after the slow start to the day.

The helicopter ride took an hour at most, and he recalled the view was mostly of water. He was shipped over to location alongside Mr. Blue and Mr. Black, who sat next to each other on the opposite side of the helicopter. Ranger accompanied them on the trip, and spent the entire flight curled up in the corner, sound asleep. The flight was uneventful, and nobody made small talk. Mr. Black, in particular, didn't move much the entire trip. He had calmly stared straight forward at the empty seat next to Mr. White. Mr. Blue sat next to the window, staring at his map. After boarding the helicopter and getting situated, Ranger had handed each of them a map of the terrain. Mr. White had surveyed the landscape in flight and determined it best to evaluate his options once on site. Instead, he recalled spending most of the flight silently focused on his firm's new product launch. Innovation was the core of everything he did; Mr. White likened a product launch to Christmas morning. The timing for this trip couldn't have been worse, but he knew from his contacts that this expedition's showrunners had a less-than-forgiving reputation, and if he declined, there would not be a second invitation. He had also invested a significant amount of time during the previous month in training. It was now or never.

He remembered the helicopter landing in a field to the north of the island. The tall grass waved in every direction as they softly touched down. All four men quickly disembarked and cleared the rotor blades. Once they were clear, the helicopter swiftly lifted and headed back the direction they came.

Ranger was the first to leave. Mr. White wasn't even sure which direction Ranger had walked; one second they were disembarking, the next they were alone in the field. He was sure Ranger was close and trying to keep out of sight. *As he should.*

The three remaining men stood in the field and watched the helicopter until it disappeared. Wasting little time, Mr. Black dropped to his knees and took inventory of his pack's contents. Mr. Blue was standing in amazement as he surveyed the terrain in all directions with a giddy smile on his face.

"Alright, gentlemen," Mr. Black began as he stood and saddled his pack into place. "Best of luck to you both. I'm headed this way," he added while pointing straight up the middle of the terrain. "None of you better follow me."

Mr. White remembered watching Mr. Black for quite some time before deciding to trek towards the hills to his left. He recalled looking back to Mr. Blue, who had chosen to go right after seeing where his two opponents were headed. Minutes later, Mr. White was scaling a hill, and on his own. He climbed for several hours before deciding to make a pit stop for a snack and bathroom break. His map indicated there was a river just ahead, so he set up shop for a meal.

It was shortly thereafter that he came across Chris. *The guy really had no idea what was going on; he just walked right up to me. It was almost too easy. If only I had reacted faster.* Mr. White had joined the expedition not convinced the prey were real; he was almost certain this would be a role-play expedition, but the deeper he got into preparation, the more his perspective began to shift. The previous twenty-four hours brought everything into focus; being reunited with the Broker in this context made everything feel real.

He had met the Broker through a mutual acquaintance over a year ago and finally received an invite in recent months. The proposal initially sounded outlandish and cruel.

"We have several offerings to choose from," the Broker began as he jotted a note down on a drink napkin, "but I've found this particular scenario has provided overly taxed individuals, such as yourself, with a much-needed flexing of other cognitive muscles."

Mr. White looked down at the napkin, read the note, and shook his head.

"Think about it," he recalled the Broker telling him over drinks. "How many people have worked for you over the years?"

Still early in his career, Mr. White already had no clue. "I don't know, several hundred."

"And what do those lives mean to you? Have you met all of them? Do you know who they are?"

"Some."

The Broker leaned in. "Let me tell you something. Call it luck, talent, or a bit of both, but you've quickly ascended to the top in a very complex game. Nearly everybody on this planet will spend the majority, if not all, of their lives living paycheck to paycheck in the pursuit of something more." He paused to take a sip from his Pimm's cup and continued. "Their pursuits are in vain. They will dedicate their lives, time, and energy to the betterment of a select few, namely individuals such as yourself. They're worker bees or cattle. Use whatever metaphor you'd like. But at the end of the day, the majority lead inconsequential lives. They find meaning and solace in building families, but all they're really doing is perpetuating the cycle."

Mr. White recalled initially finding the Broker's explanation exceedingly cynical. He, of course, had no personal connection to the vast majority of his direct reports, and was well aware of his reputation as a manager. But all of his employees had a choice, or at least the perception of choice, whether they came to work each day. The Broker's proposal was something completely different. *Except when evaluating the concept of choice. True, people cannot show up to work, but then they would default on their obligations. Perhaps the Broker is right, the cycle is perpetual and more black-and-white than I realized.*

"People will live and die under your watch as CEO," the Broker continued, "on aggregate, you will be none the wiser. What we offer is no different, we simply extract utility."

The Broker's remarks weren't untrue, he recalled, and he did find the overall concept eerily insatiable. Maybe it was driven from a darker subconscious he had refused to acknowledge, or a simple desire to conquer something new. He wasn't sure, but the urge was real.

What happened next didn't take long. The Broker assured him of zero ramifications and absolute secrecy. "To track and hunt this planet's apex predator will be unlike any challenge you've faced before."

Mr. White put his name on the list shortly thereafter.

The Broker wasn't wrong; the adrenaline rush of the recent chase felt like rocket fuel had been injected into his veins. *That was one hell of a risk, though,* he thought to himself as he slowly walked to the river edge. He knew the Kate girl had spotted him but was impressed by how quickly she and the others reacted. To his surprise, the fake trail had worked to perfection and had given him an edge; he wasn't even sure he did it right. But as he descended farther down the hill, he became suspicious that they had evaded him and were actually still uphill. It was a gamble that left him tense until he spotted the crew making their way down the hill following the fake trail. The plan had worked, and the advantage was his, if only his shot had hit the target. The overall approach down to the river edge left something to be desired. Walking to the edge of the water, he looked down at the mist below. They had leapt right off the edge and down into the river below. *I wonder who wins if they all jump to their deaths?*

***

The Broker sat back in his chair in the control room. In front of him, five techs sat behind computer screens typing while talking into headsets wrapped around their heads from ear to ear. The front wall of the control room was covered in a series of giant video screens; stacked on the left and right edges, eighty inches each. In the middle was a single large screen, which currently displayed a digital map of the terrain with six colored "X" marks. A White X to the center-left, a Black X in the middle a bit north of the white, a Blue X along the far-right edge of the map, and three Red Xs clustered just to the right of the White X.

"What was the time?" the Broker asked one of the techs while not breaking his gaze from the main screen.

"Contact at 31:03 dot 40, sir," a tech responded.

"Mark it in the logs." The Broker leaned forward, reflecting on the events that had just unfolded on the hills. "Bring up the body cam, please."

Almost immediately, a live view from Mr. White's chest made up the large middle screen.

"And back it up to contact." The screen rewound. There were moments of pause and significant movement. From time to time, the Broker caught sight of the prey as they moved quickly to evade. "Stop, right there." The Broker stood and looked at the screen, which showed Mr. White standing over a fire and Chris slowly walking toward him. "Freeze it right there and mark."

"Done," replied another tech.

"And proceed," the Broker said as he watched the events unfold. Chris walked up from a distance, pausing, Mr. White backing up, reaching down, loading, and then firing at Chris. "Pause again. Time?"

"12.7 seconds, sir."

That was too slow. The Broker looked over at the tech to his farthest left. "Please mark the training logs of an initial response time of 12.7, and let's make sure that's corrected as part of the next training cycle. I also want to bring his training coordinator up for review." The Broker looked to his far-right. "Vectors, please."

A tech to the far right ran his finger across his screen, then looked over at the Broker. "Sufficient velocity, aim was off by 2.735 degrees. The strike after the fake trail clipped subject Chris on the shoulder. Distance estimates a main torso miss by 1.325 degrees."

The Broker leaned back in his chair. *We need to clean up our preparation practices. Mr. White had all day to take aim and fire both of those misses. These folks are paying us too much to miss like that.*

Ring. Ring.

Leaning forward, the Broker picked up a red telephone. "Yes?" He waited for a moment and listened to the other end. "Okay, thank you." He hung up the phone. He leaned back in his chair with slight satisfaction. "Confirmed, refresh the board, please."

***

Mr. White leaned close to the rocky edge, where the river dropped off into the river below. *There isn't a chance in hell I'm jumping. I'll have to take the long way.* Mr. White turned around and began to march toward the tree line.

Buzz. Buzz.

Mr. White looked down at his wrist. The screen flashed an update.

Scoreboard Update.
Mr. White - 200 Points
Mr. Blue - 0 Points
Mr. Black - 0 Points

"200?" he whispered to himself, looking down at his watch. He knew he had clipped Chris in the woods but thought that was it. He recalled firing a shot as they jumped off the edge but was sure it missed high and hit the trees on the far side. "I guess not," Mr. White muttered as he shrugged and began to make his way down the hill.

30:45:33

Kate burst through the water's surface, gasping for air. The current immediately thrust her back down as she fought for a second breath. Kicking and pulling with everything her arms and legs could give, she heaved forward, cresting the waterline again. This time she was able to keep her head above water. The current was significantly stronger than the river above and continued to pull and toss her with ease. Veering around in all directions, she attempted to find the closest shoreline. The water dunked her again. Kicking up, she emerged, spitting and coughing water from her mouth. The current showed no signs of letting up. Unable to touch the bottom of the river, she continued to kick. Each moment, her legs and arms burned more than the last. *I need to get to shore, fast.*

Kate surveyed both sides of the river. Both banks were dominated by densely grown trees. However, she determined the left was more advantageous as she spotted a downed tree hanging over the river's edge. Kicking as hard as she could, she made her way to the left. The current remained strong as the tree quickly drew closer. *I have one shot at this.* She slowly positioned herself in line with the tree. Bobbing up and down, she fought to keep her line of sight forward. With her legs about to give out, she slowed the kicking just enough to keep her head above water. The tree grew closer.

In one single and abrupt motion, Kate bobbed in the water, kicked hard and launched herself up just as the tree came into range. With a thud, she struck the trunk and grasped it with both hands. The current continued to push her lower body under the tree as she struggled to create leverage on the slippery trunk, and water flowed around and over her shoulders. Finding a groove on the backside, she dug her fingers in and pulled. Almost instantly, her body lifted from the water. Pushing up, she braced her stomach on the trunk and locked her elbows for balance. Her knees and feet remained in the water. Lifting her left leg up and over the trunk, she straddled the log and secured her position. Pausing, she frantically tried to catch her breath. Pushing her hair away from her face, Kate began to survey the river. *Where are they?*

She wasn't entirely sure how she had survived the jump. Everything had happened so fast. She remembered spotting the unknown man in the tree line, thanks to the sunlight refracting off of his watch. The next thing she remembered was hitting the icy water below. She recalled the current carrying her into a rock or two as she moved downstream. One collision in particular left its mark. Reaching up, she rubbed her temple in the hope that it would ease the tension. Lowering her hand, she found the diluted refinements of blood washing off her fingers. *I can see fine, balance is fine, I should be okay.*

Kate quickly surveyed the river for any sign of her crew. *Have they already passed this point? I don't remember seeing them at all.* The sun rays provided quick warmth on her shoulders as her body continued to tremble. Holding her balance, she continued to frantically scan the surface of the water, searching for any sign of Chris or Kevin.

In a split second, she caught something out of place to her right. Focusing her gaze, she spotted a bobbing object; it was Kevin, and he was surprisingly close to the branch. "Hey!" she shouted as he approached. Kevin immediately turned his head; his arms remained below the surface, and he didn't say anything, only grimaced and began to drift her direction.

Kate shifted her weight and locked her position with her legs. Turning her body, she prepared both arms to extract him from the water. Kevin drew closer. The current, still rough, wouldn't accommodate an easy maneuver, similar to her own experience; they would have one shot.

A few feet away from Kate, Kevin raised his arms into the air and gritted his teeth. Reaching down, Kate swung to grab him. Their arms met, but their wet grip didn't hold. Their hands quickly slipped apart. *No you don't.*

Kevin smacked into the log and was briefly slowed. Reaching down, Kate grabbed his shirt and left arm. *Got you.* "C'mon Kevin, reach up, I can't hold this," she said while holding on to him with all her strength.

Reaching up, Kevin grabbed the log and her thigh. Breathing heavily, Kate heaved, and his upper body came up and over the log. The lower half of his body remained in the water, but his grip was sound. Kate looked him over. *I don't see any blood.* "You okay, Kevin?"

He continued to clutch the log and grimace.

"Hey! Look at me, are you okay? Can you hear me?"

Grinding his teeth, he looked up at her and shook his head. "My leg." He paused and spat out a mouthful of water. "I need to get out of here."

Kate looked down for his legs. They were both still underwater; however, she could tell from his facial expressions that something wasn't right. Nodding, she reached for Kevin. "Alright, let's get you to shore."

Slowly, Kate shimmied backward. One hand was used for balance, and the other gripped Kevin's shirt. Down in the water, Kevin gripped the log and Kate's leg. After several painstaking minutes, Kate looked down at the water. *I can see the bottom, and the current doesn't look too bad.* In a gamble, Kate dismounted from the log and jumped in. She was immediately shocked all over by the cold; however, her gamble had paid off, as the water was only a few feet deep. Lunging forward, she turned Kevin around, positioned him against her chest, locked her arms around his armpits, and began to pull him to shore. Kevin didn't say a word, as he pushed toward the shore using one leg.

As they approached the shore, Kate was able to make out a long black object protruding from Kevin's left leg. *Dammit, he's hit.* Near the shore, she pulled him up and, in a pivot, threw his arm over her shoulder and helped carry him to the river's edge. Surveying the shore, Kate realized how lucky they were. They had managed to find one of the few places along the river's edge where one could exit with relative ease.

Making shore, Kate dragged Kevin away from the edge and helped him find a seat at the base of a tree, covered in the shade. Catching her breath, Kate went down on both knees and began to examine Kevin's leg. A sleek black arrow ran through his left calf. The strike looked relatively clean. It didn't appear to have struck the bone, though she wasn't sure, and the blood loss had slowed in the cold water.

"Alright, we need to get this out of you," she said while touching the shaft of the arrow.

Kevin grimaced. "Ahh, don't touch that."

"We need to get this removed, and we need to clean the wound."

"Yea, I hear you, but we need a better surface. We need tools or something. If you rip this out as is, it'll cause more damage. Then I'm screwed."

Kate knew Kevin was right. The barbs were made of a sharp fiberglass-type material, and the arrowhead had a serrated tip. Removing from either side would likely cause more damage. *We might not have a choice. If this gets infected, he will lose his leg. Kate looked around the river edge. Is there a better surface to do this? Is there anything I can use?*

"Hey guys!" a voice shouted from afar.

Kevin and Kate looked up and gazed across the river. In the distance, on the other side of the river, stood Chris, waving with both hands.

Kate waved her hand back at him. "We need help!"

Chris shook his head and motioned for them to move downriver.

Kate turned back to Kevin. "Think you can walk?"

"Yeah, for a bit," Kevin replied as he began to stand, using the tree as a crutch. "Interesting that he's on the same side we jumped from," Kevin began. "I didn't see him jump, did you?"

"No." Kate paused. "I didn't."

30:28:17

Keeping close to the tree line to take advantage of the shade, Kate and Kevin worked their way along the riverbank. Kate surmised the trees might also provide quick cover should the unnamed assailant show up again, though Kate knew if he did, they wouldn't be able to escape given Kevin's condition. Chris continued to follow on the other side of the river, occasionally pointing forward or into the woods; Kate and Kevin weren't always sure what he was trying to communicate, but it was clear he wanted them to continue following the river.

Their pace was slow as Kevin hobbled on one foot, using Kate as a crutch. The bleeding around the entry and exit wounds had mostly stopped, but Kevin had to be careful with each step so as not to cut his other leg on the protruding arrowhead or catch a tree with the other end of the arrow. He did that once within his first few steps, and the bend from the shaft was so excruciating that his legs gave out and he collapsed on the spot. It wasn't just the pain from within, but also a genuine loss of strength and restrictive movements in his leg that slowed his pace. *Is this because of the arrow, or is it permanent?*

After a short while, Kate and Kevin emerged from the trees into a large field. The terrain and growth were similar to the area they had woken in earlier in the day. To their left, the tree line swept across the field for several miles, and then joined another set of large rolling foothills in the distance. To the right, the river remained thirty feet across, but the current's strength appeared to have significantly dissipated. Chris, who continued to wave and march forward, was still surrounded by trees. The sun quickly returned and beat unforgivingly on their skin.

"How much longer until the sun is gone?" Kevin asked.

"Not sure," Kate began while peering toward the general location of the sun. "Quite a while though. At least four, maybe five more hours. Once it goes below the hill, we'll have another hour or two where we won't have the sun on us, but it also won't be dark. We'll need to make moves then."

"Word. Hey, at least you were right about that tree line and field, here we are," Kevin added.

"Yeah, just hoping we're able to cross the river sometime soon."

"Hey!" Chris shouted from the other side, pointing to a bend in the river.

"Wonder what he wants now?" Kevin muttered.

Kate looked back at Kevin, who was panting heavily and dripping with sweat. "Need to rest?" Kate asked.

"No, I'm good."

"Then let's go find out," Kate said as she guided Kevin forward across the field.

Moments later, it became obvious to Kevin and Kate why Chris was yelling. Around the bend, only a few hundred feet away, stood an old wooden bridge that connected both sides of the river. More importantly, the tree line abruptly dissipated on Chris' side of the river, and a large field emerged with multiple manmade structures nearby. Kate and Kevin quickly turned their path toward the river's edge to get a better look.

Across the field stood three old structures. The one closest to the tree line was clearly a barn, though there were several holes in the roof and side, and the color was a faded dark brown. A hundred feet to the left was a two-story farmhouse. The exterior was still white with a large porch wrapping the two sides of the exterior they could see. The overall design was Victorian. The house easily had several rooms and likely provided shelter for several individuals during its prime. To the far right along the far riverbank stood a mill. Rudimentary in design, the mill looked long abandoned, as was evident by the motionless large wooden wheel still partially submerged in the river.

"Think anybody lives there?" Kevin asked.

"I hope so. Maybe they have a phone or a radio," Kate responded. She paused for a moment and gave the buildings a second glance before nudging Kevin back on pace toward the bridge. As they approached the bridge, Chris ran over to them. The smile on his face quickly turned to shock.

"Jesus, Kevin, that looks like hell."

"Good to see you too," Kevin replied as Chris walked over to assist Kate in moving him.

Chris gestured for Kate to stop for a moment. He knelt down and inspected Kevin's leg. "We need to get this cleaned out," Chris began as he moved his hands in position around Kevin's wound.

"I'm aware," Kevin said as he rolled his head. "You think I could lose it?"

"Not sure. Maybe. I'm more concerned about infection or blood poisoning, especially out here with no help," Chris continued as he looked closer at the wound. "This is going to hurt a bit, but I need to check something." Grabbing Kevin's leg, he began to push above and below the arrow on his tibia. "Any pain?"

Kevin grimaced. "Not so much where you're pushing, but touching my leg in general hurts a lot. Please hurry up."

Chris withdrew his hands. "Can you put weight on it?"

"More or less."

"Alright, I don't think it's broken, but I can't be sure until I get in there."

"What do you mean by 'get in there?'" Kevin asked.

Chris looked over at Kate, who knew exactly what he was about to say. "We must get that arrow out. Leaving it in isn't an option. We should go over to that house and see if there's anybody who can help us. If they happen to have a radio or phone, we'll get you to an ER, but if not, we need to have a serious discussion about what happens next."

Kevin glared silently for a few moments before he finally realized Chris and Kate's genuine concern. "Get me out of the sun," Kevin grunted as he began to push forward.

Step by step, the crew made their way to the old wooden bridge. By Kate's estimation, the bridge was at least a century old, and creaked and swayed with each step they took. The primary supports were made of stone, and the body of the bridge was wood, most likely local hemlock. The crossing took a few minutes as Kevin braced against Kate and Chris while taking short steps to avoid having the arrow in his leg make contact with any part of the structure.

On the other side of the river, the crew got a better look at the terrain. Behind the barn was a large field with dense growth of local plant life and wheat scattered throughout. They were on a small farm. A farm that hadn't been operational in a very long time, and from the looks of it hadn't come into human contact for equally as long. There were no signs of life, machinery, or power. They were alone.

"So much for the ER," Kevin muttered.

"How ya holding up?" Chris asked.

"Will need a rest soon."

"I think we should make for the house. Maybe there's something inside we could use," Chris concluded. Leaving Kevin's side, he began to forge forward. "I'll go ahead and scope out the house."

"I think we should stick together," Kevin replied, looking up at Kate with a suspicious glare.

"Yea, we're not that far, let's get Kevin inside, and then we can explore," Kate added.

Chris shrugged his shoulders and returned to Kevin's side. "Suit yourselves." Together they made their way to the farmhouse. There were remnants of an old path system leading between the structures and from the bridge to the house. The path was mostly overgrown, but the deposits of small white rocks and gravel were still visible. Following the trail for a few more moments, they arrived at the house. Kate and Chris lifted Kevin up two wooden steps and onto the porch of the farmhouse. Gesturing for a pause, Chris left Kevin's side, walked to the front door, and gently turned the handle. "It's open."

The handle creaked as Chris turned it to the right, and upon hearing a click, he pushed the door open. Looking back and Kevin and Kate, he held his hand up, indicating for them to wait. "Hello?" Chris shouted into the house. There was no answer. After a few seconds of silence, Chris walked into the house, looked around, and then disappeared to the right behind the open door. Creaking sounds came from within the as Chris inspected the house.

"Got anything?" Kate shouted into the house.

"Nope, come on in," Chris replied.

Kate and Kevin walked slowly through the open door to find a mostly empty house. The wood floors were covered in dust, a large staircase to the second floor occupied the main entryway, and the nearby rooms were void of furniture. Chris came back and joined them. "All the rooms are empty."

"Did you find the kitchen?" Kevin asked.

"Not yet, let's try over here." Chris pointed to an unexplored room to the left. As the crew rounded the corner into the new room, they found Chris' intuition was spot on. The kitchen was small and unfortunately had no equipment or utilities of any kind. There was a small sink with no faucet along the left wall near a window, and a single wooden table in the center of the room.

"Let's get you up here," Kate said to Kevin as she gestured for him to sit on the table. Kevin hobbled over to it, and with Kate and Chris' help, he was hoisted onto the surface.

Kate walked over to the sink. "Where do you think they got their water?"

"Probably the river," Chris replied as he knelt down to examine Kevin's wound. "I'm sorry, Kevin, but we need to get this out immediately."

"I'm aware of that," Kevin said with angry sarcasm. "And how do we do that without any tools?"

"I'm not sure," Chris replied as he stood and stared around the room. He walked over to the cabinets and drawers, opening each and then moving on. Nothing.

"What about the barn?" Kate interjected.

"That's actually not a bad idea," replied Chris. "You okay staying with him while I check it out?"

"You both should go," Kevin replied.

"No, I really think one of us should stay here with you," Chris replied. "The last thing we need is for you to pass out and fall off the table or something."

There was a short pause. Kate looked at Kevin, who was clearly reluctant. "He's right," she said while looking back at Chris. "You go check out the barn, I'll stay with Kevin."

"Be right back," Chris said as he jogged out of the room.

Kate and Kevin patiently waited in silence for Chris to return. Neither was willing to mention Kevin's current skepticism toward this plan. It was too late. Chris was gone, and he was by himself again. He would either come back and help them or he wouldn't.

***

Kate wasn't entirely sure how much time had passed. She forgot to take note of her watch when Chris left, but she guessed it had been at least fifteen minutes. "Should I go take a look where he is?" she asked Kevin.

"Give him a few more minutes."

Pacing the room, Kate decided to look for Chris out a window on the opposite side of the house. She made her way toward the front door, aiming for the room just beyond. In a sudden burst, Chris emerged through the front door with several objects in hand. "Hey!" he said, panting.

Startled, Kate jumped back. "Jesus, you scared me."

"Sorry about that. Took a little longer than I expected."

"Any luck?"

"See for yourself," Chris replied as he held up a small rusted saw in his right hand, and a bucket with bits of tinder inside.

"What's that for?" Kate gestured toward the bucket.

"Kevin's not going to be happy." Chris started walking toward the kitchen. "But this needs to happen."

Chris and Kate entered the kitchen to find Kevin hadn't moved an inch. He looked over at them and then down at the contents in Chris' hands.

"Not exactly Christmas," Kevin said apprehensively.

Chris walked up and placed the saw and bucket on the table next to Kevin, and then looked up at him. "I can't guarantee this will work, but we have to try," he said.

Kevin looked over at Kate, who nodded. "Let's get this over with. What do you need me to do?"

"Bring your leg up and roll onto your stomach."

Kevin slowly pivoted and followed Chris' instructions.

Chris gestured for Kate to come over. "Alright, we need to carefully bring his leg over to the edge."

Sliding his leg slowly into place, Chris waved for Kate to assist. "Put your hands here, and here," Chris said while pointing to positions before and after the arrow's entry point. "Don't let him move."

Kate nodded.

"Okay. Kevin, I've lined your leg up with the edge of the table, so the arrow is now running perpendicular to the surface. I'm going to go below the table line and saw off the arrowhead."

"Good God." Kevin rolled his head back and stared at the far wall.

"I got the arrow tight against the wood here, so the overall strain on your leg should be minimized as much as possible. You ready?"

Kate pressed down on Kevin's leg with her weight and awaited his approval.

"Let's get this over with," Kevin muttered.

Chris took a deep breath, clenched the rusted saw in his hand, and steadily thrust back and forth against the arrow's shaft. Kevin grimaced and clenched his leg muscles. Kate added pressure to his leg to keep it from moving. Back and forth, Chris worked on the arrow. It took a few strokes to break through the exterior of the shaft, but once through, Chris made it to the other side in fewer than ten strokes. Kevin continued to breathe heavily as the blade neared the arrow's other edge. Hitting a snag on the final edge of the arrow, Chris paused and adjusted his sawing angle.

"Just do it!" Kate shouted down at Chris.

Chris adjusted to a squatting position, twisted the end of the arrow, braced his leverage on Kevin's leg, and drove the saw into the remaining bit of fiberglass. Kevin grit his teeth and began to breathe harder.

Snap. Slip.

In sequential moves, Chris severed the head of the arrow from the shaft and removed the arrow from Kevin's calf. Kevin let out a grunt of pain. Quickly moving, Chris took off his shirt and pressed the cloth onto the wound as blood poured from Kevin's leg. "Hold here, hard." Chris gestured to Kate, who repositioned herself and applied pressure to Kevin's leg.

"Is it over?" Kevin gasped.

"Not quite," Chris replied. "We have to stop the bleeding."

Stepping back from the table, Chris picked up the pail and set it in the sink. He returned to Kate's side. "Matches," he said in a stern tone.

"Back pocket," she said while keeping her focus on Kevin's leg. "Left."

Chris reached into Kate's back pocket and removed the matches. He inspected the pack. *Just as I hoped, waterproof.* He walked back to the bucket, lit a match and applied it to the tinder near the bottom. Smoke emerged from the bucket, but the fire didn't take. Chris took out a second match and tried again. This time, he applied the flame to a few spots and lightly blew on the smoking embers. In a quick burst, a fire erupted from the bucket. Chris smiled in satisfaction but quickly returned to Kate, knowing he had little time.

Chris returned to Kevin's side, placed the matches next to Kate, and detached the metal canteen from his belt. He gestured for Kate to remove the shirt from the wound. She quickly complied and revealed Kevin's blood-soaked leg while grabbing the matches and putting them back in her pocket. *He'll require rehab, but not as bad as I thought.* Chris leaned in and poured water from the canteen onto Kevin's wound. "Looks clean," Chris said as he stood and gestured for Kate to hand him the t-shirt. He quickly wrung it, turned and, in a quick tug, ripped off one of the sleeves. He flipped the shirt over and ripped off the other sleeve. Shifting his stance, he tossed Kate what remained and gestured for her to reapply pressure to Kevin's leg. Meanwhile, Chris took the two short sleeves, set one inside the other so they overlapped, and carefully shimmied the cloth over Kevin's foot and up the base of his shin. "We'll use this once we're done. The sleeves still have some elasticity, should work nicely." Chris left the sleeves loose on Kevin's shin and walked back to the flaming bucket.

At the sink, Chris carefully set the empty canteen into the fire with the top end edged away from the flames. "Kate," Chris said as he pointed to the arrow he had just removed from Kevin's leg, "use the shaft."

Kate understood precisely what Chris wanted and reached over with her left hand and grabbed the arrow. Carefully leaning forward, she slid the shaft to Kevin. "Put this in your mouth."

"What, why?" Kevin replied in confusion.

"You have an open wound, and it's bleeding everywhere. We need to stop the bleeding."

Kevin looked at the arrow. There were still remnants of blood and flesh on the shaft. He looked over at Chris, standing over the bucket engulfed in flames, and realized what was happening. "No way, Kate!" he yelled.

"Shut up and bite, we don't have time for this," she insisted.

Kevin realized she was serious, looked back at the arrow, and put it between his teeth just as Chris carefully removed the canteen with his fingertips and walked toward Kevin.

"Sorry, bud, this is going to really hurt," Chris said as he nodded at Kate, who immediately removed the shirt from his leg and wiped the blood with her hand. In a fluid motion, Chris applied the scolding metal canteen to Kevin's leg and pressed.

Kevin grimaced and bit down hard on the arrow. His body squirmed as Chris held the canteen to his leg. His flesh sizzled, and light smoke rose from the base of the canteen. Chris waited a few seconds and then withdrew the canteen. He looked down at the wound and blew lightly. Smoke continued to rise from the singed hair around Kevin's would. Looking up at Kevin, Chris smiled. "Nice job," he said and walked back to the bucket.

Kevin, breathing heavily, removed the arrow from his mouth. "How'd it go?"

"Perfect," Kate replied. "Now we just need to get the other side."

Kevin groaned and smacked his forehead down on the table in frustration.

Chris stood over the fire, waiting for the canteen to reheat. While waiting, Kate softly shifted Kevin's calf off the table so he wouldn't have to roll over again. "This side isn't as bad," she said to Kevin as she pressed on the wound with the bloody shirt.

Moments later, Chris removed the canteen from the bucket again with his fingertips and walked toward Kevin, who knew what was coming and put the arrow back in his mouth. "Last time, bud," Chris said as he knelt down, looked up at Kevin's leg from below, and carefully applied the canteen to his leg for a second time. The process only lasted a few seconds, but to Kevin it was an eternity.

When satisfied, Chris removed the canteen from Kevin's leg and set it on the table. He softly blew on Kevin's leg from below and nodded at Kate.

"Now is it over?" Kevin asked as he spat the arrow out of his mouth.

Chris stood, carefully took the shirt sleeves around Kevin's shin, and pulled them over the wounds on both sides. The fit was snug.

"Yes," Kate said, "you did great." Taking leave, Kate set the bloody shirt on the table next to the rusty saw, stepped out of the room, and headed toward the front door to get some air. She knew Kevin would be okay. Taking a deep breath, she walked around the room, running her hand on the bottom of the stairway banister. For the first time all day, relief took over. They were reunited with Chris, Kevin would walk again, and the farm provided some shelter and protection. They still needed to figure out their food situation, but things were now under control. Taking a deep breath, she walked toward the front window.

Gasping, she spun and dropped to her knees. Her moment of serenity was over, and adrenaline had returned to her veins. She began to breathe harder but knew she had to take control. Inhaling a few deep breaths, she crouched, turned around, and carefully inched up and peered through the window next to the door. Her heart sank. Less than a hundred meters away, a young man wearing a white watch, with a bow ready in hand, was carefully approaching the farmhouse.

30:15:52

M r. White followed the river's edge to the farm. Shortly after he had chased the prey over the waterfall, he recalled from his map that the river ran next to an old farming establishment. Pulling the map from his back pocket, he quickly confirmed the farm was approximately a mile away. *Follow the river downhill until the terrain opens up to a field. The farm will be right by a bend in the river.* He knew if the prey had survived the fall, they likely wouldn't venture too far from the water source, especially if he had in fact injured one of them, which meant they would likely come across the farm and possibly stop.

He spent the next half hour descending the hill. The slight decline of the terrain enabled him to keep a brisk pace without overly straining his lungs. He remained mindful of the protruding tree roots and rocky terrain, none of which gave him pause to slow his pace. In short order he made the bottom of the hill and broke through to the open field. He crouched along the tree line and surveyed the field in front of him. A barn stood to his right, a white farmhouse straight ahead, and a mill to his far left near the river's bend.

He waited a few moments to see if there was any movement. *Nothing.* He stood, pulled the map from his back pocket, and reviewed the terrain. *Where else would they have gone?* He scratched his cheek and wiped the sweat from his forehead.

While surveying the map, Mr. White caught a faint whiff of smoke. Looking to his right, he didn't see anything coming from the farm or nearby fields. Shifting his gaze to the farmhouse, he caught the sight of a small white flume rising from the side of the house; it was very faint, but definitely there. He smiled and folded the map.

Reaching into the pack on his shoulders, he carefully removed an arrow and softly placed it into position on the bow. Holding everything in one hand, he tapped his side to confirm his knife was still in position on his belt. *There's three of them, and one of me. One of them is injured, possibly two. The Asian guy isn't of concern, but together in small quarters, they could potentially take me.* He crouched and continued to survey the white house. *I need to disable one of them, get them separated, and then I'll be all set.* He tapped the knife on his hip again. *That's the best I'm going to do without compromising the element of surprise.*

He stood slowly and began walking softly toward the house, loaded bow in hand.

29:04:16

Kate frantically crawled back to the kitchen. Chris stood next to the table talking to Kevin, who was sitting up and in better spirits. They were making small talk when she crashed into the kitchen. She rolled around the corner wall and stood, breathing heavily and frantically evaluating their options.

"What's going on?" Kevin asked.

"Shh," Kate replied while holding her index finger to her lips.

Chris immediately ducked and moved toward Kate.

"We have company," she whispered to him.

"Where?"

"Front door. Maybe a hundred feet. He's walking this way."

Chris nodded and gestured for her to come over to where Kevin sat. Keeping low, they both made their way across the room toward Kevin, who continued to sit on the table. He was clearly frozen by how quickly their fortunes had turned.

Back at the table, Chris evaluated their surroundings. He moved from the table toward a door at the back of the kitchen. Quickly turning the knob and pushing the door ajar, he disappeared into the room nestled off the back of the house. Seconds later, he reemerged and made his way back to Kate and Kevin.

"We need to draw him in close. As long as he can pull an arrow on us, we're at a disadvantage," Chris began.

"What do we do?" Kate whispered.

"I have a plan. This way," he replied as he gestured for them to follow him into the back room.

29:02:22

M r. White slowly approached the farmhouse from the side. Edging up against the exterior, he peered through the side window. The interior was barren, and there was no sight of the prey, though there was a hint of smoke in the air, and he had clearly found its source. He paused and removed his pack and set it next to the porch. The bag wouldn't provide any utility in his pursuit; if anything, it would slow him down. He set the arrow in hand for a quick shot and inched toward the front door. Remaining calm and low, he took a deep breath.

He slowly pivoted to the front door, making sure to avoid the small path of loose stones and gravel leading from the river to the front porch. He quietly ascended the first step, then second. Approaching the open front door, he peered through the nearby window and spotted movement inside to his left. Quickly shifting, he caught a glimpse of Kate near the back wall. *Got you.* In a swift motion, he lined up his arrow and fired.

29:03:36

C hris quietly assisted Kevin as he climbed out the window of the back room. He gestured for Kevin to stay quiet. Kevin eased onto the grass and kept his body tight against the house.

Chris looked back at Kate. "We have one shot at getting him in the front door. If he doesn't bite, this doesn't end well, especially for Kevin," he whispered. Kate nodded, clearly understanding the stakes and how the next sixty seconds likely meant life or death.

Once Kevin was settled outside, Chris motioned for Kate to follow him back into the kitchen. Pointing toward the opening that bridged the house's entryway with the kitchen, he began to brief Kate. "I need you to catch his attention. If you stand on the corner closest to this spot, on the left, you'll minimize your exposure." Chris paused and looked back at the room. "I need you to draw him into this room. Once he's fired, and hopefully, it's only once, draw him to the back room. I'm going to position myself at the door around the corner," he said pointing to the left. "Once you draw him into that back room, I want you to get the hell out of here, grab Kevin, and make your way across the field to the mill."

"How will I know when it's safe to move?" Kate asked.

"You'll hear it." Chris smiled. He gestured back to the kitchen entryway. "Protect your head, don't give him a clean shot. Keep quiet, and shift as you hear him draw. I've seen him fire a few times now, and he tends to draw up and away from his targets."

    Kate nodded, and they both moved into position.

29:01:06

Mr. White edged forward, drew his arrow, and released. The arrow ripped through the air and struck the far wall to the left, plunging deeply into a wooden window frame. *How the hell did I miss? She had her back to me. Did she move?* Mr. White didn't have time to determine what exactly had happened; all he knew was he missed, and the prey were likely alerted to his presence. He quickly turned and tossed his bow into the grass near his pack, removed the knife from his hip, snapped it open, and entered the house.

Keeping alert, Mr. White swiftly entered, peering in all directions. He made his way toward what appeared to be a kitchen to the left of the entrance. Suddenly, Kate popped her head around the corner and looked directly at him. She pushed back from the wall and began to run. Mr. White rounded the corner just in time to see her enter a room near the rear of the kitchen. There was no sight of the other two prey, but the table in the middle and surrounding floor were covered in blood. Mr. White picked up his pace and headed toward the wall just left of the back-room entrance. He peered laterally through the doorway from a distance to ensure there wasn't anybody on the far side waiting for him; he remembered that from training. The wall looked clear.

Taking one step further, he cautiously paused at the doorframe and waited. Following a sudden thud from inside the room, Mr. White decided to make his move. In a fluid shift, he pushed off from the wall and swiftly stepped inside. As he entered the room, he spotted the girl, Kate, climbing through a window at the back of the room and exiting the house. Dammit. Turning around to course correct, he was too late. Chris emerged from behind the door, struck Mr. White's hand and sent his knife to the floor, and then shoved him against the wall. Mr. White swung his knee forward and sent Chris off balance, which bought him just enough time to push off from the wall and reset his stance.

Bringing his arms into a boxing position, Mr. White shifted his stance and marched toward Chris. Noticing the flesh wound from his arrow strike earlier in the day, Mr. White launched toward Chris, pinning him against the wall, and pounded on Chris' shoulder. Chris shifted his arms and went for Mr. White's face, who saw the move coming and blocked it with his forearm. Mr. White's block put an end to the assault on Chris' shoulder. Using both hands, Chris pushed Mr. White back and ran for the kitchen. Mr. White regained his balance, stopped to pick up his army knife from the floor, and then took off after Chris.

* * *

The commotion inside the house was difficult to decipher. Kate paused and contemplated going back inside to help Chris, but she knew her role was equally important. *Get Kevin to safety and create distance between you two and the attacker.* Looking down at Kevin, she motioned to him that it was time to move. Reaching down, Kate helped lift Kevin to his feet and led him around the edge of the house. She had no clue how Chris was faring, but she knew if he lost, they were next.

The mill was less than half a football field from the house. It looked farther away when they initially came upon the farm, but it became clear to Kate that the distance had been skewed by their approach and how the river bent around it. Kate looked back at Kevin and listened one more time into the house; she heard loud footsteps, as if somebody was running. "Now," she whispered.

Leading the way toward the mill, Kate pulled Kevin as fast as he could hobble. She carefully surveyed their surroundings as they sped forward; she didn't think the assailant could have seen them, but she wasn't sure. Several strides later, they were already too far from the house to hear the struggle.

Less than thirty seconds later, Kate and Kevin arrived at the mill. Not concerned about finding a door, they ran along the edge of the structure and out of view of the house. Catching her breath, Kate helped Kevin take a seat against the mill. The grass ran tall around the side, and Kevin nearly disappeared into the thicket. The sound of their movements was drowned out by the river, flowing less than ten feet from where Kevin sat. "Stay here," she said.

***

Chris raced through the kitchen and around the left corner toward the entryway of the house. His assailant followed close behind. After rounding the corner, Chris paused and stepped forward into the middle of the entryway. Seconds later, he was face-to-face with his adversary, who feverishly lunged his knife at Chris' torso and missed. Taking a step back, Chris shifted to the right, and the man paused his attack and reset. They glared into each other's eyes. The man smiled at Chris, lunged forward with his knife, and missed again.

Adjusting position, the two men paced the room, eyes locked, breathing heavily, and waited for each other to make a move. Raising his left hand, the man motioned for Chris to attack. Chris shifted back and to the left, and the man turned his body as well. In a quick burst, Chris moved forward, ducking beneath the man's counterstrike, and drove his shoulder under his armpit. The knife swung from behind his head as Chris forced the man toward the wall. They both slammed hard into the wood. Shifting his arms down, the man lunged for Chris' neck and began to squeeze.

Chris knew he was about to lose his leverage, and in a quick motion, he turned and lunged his forehead at the nose of the other man. The man screamed as blood gushed from his nose. Chris struck him again. Blood splattered both of their faces, the assailant's nose clearly broken. Dizzy from the assault, Chris didn't have time to recover. He shifted and went for the knife in the man's hand and pressed both of his thumbs into the man's wrist. The blade clanked on the floor as the man dropped the knife and howled.

Free of the knife, the assailant shifted and grabbed Chris by the hair. The grip was sharp as he yanked his hair taut. Looking down, Chris kicked the knife across the room and heaved his weight into the man again. With a crashing thud, they both struck the wall for a second time. The man gasped for air and released his grip on Chris' hair. *He's starting to give out.*

In a second motion, Chris plunged his fist into the man's abdomen. The man immediately released Chris and gasped for air. *This is it.* Chris struck him again from the side. Having the wind knocked out of him, the man could barely stand as he frantically shifted his defensive stance. With a jerk, Chris grabbed the man by the left wrist, pulled him away from the wall, and pushed him toward the window next to the front door. As the man stumbled forward, Chris applied a second blow and sent him hurtling through the glass.

***

With a sudden crash, a body flew through the front window of the farmhouse as Kate watched. The body didn't look like Chris, but she wasn't sure. Moments later, the individual used the porch railing to crawl up; it was definitely the man with the white watch. Back at the front door, Chris emerged from the house. He looked winded but had no problem standing upright.

The man lunged at Chris, who quickly sidestepped the attack just in time to see the man strike the edge of the door frame with his leading shoulder. Chris shifted toward the man, who blindly swung and didn't miss the second time, striking Chris in the chin. Chris stumbled back, and as he looked up to recover, the man lunged again.

Kate watched anxiously as the two men rolled off the porch and began to feverishly strike each other in the grass. Kate grew concerned about Chris and debated whether to run over and help. *By the time I get there, it will be over, and I'd also be giving up our position.* She decided to let the fight play out a bit further.

Rolling around on the ground, the assailant gained leverage on Chris and rolled him onto his back. Chris was pinned. The man reached down with both hands and began to squeeze Chris' neck. *Oh, God. No.*

Kate didn't see exactly how it happened, but in a swift motion, Chris lifted his left hand and drove something into the assailant's neck. The man quickly toppled over and clutched his throat. Lying on the ground for a moment, Chris caught his breath and sat up. The man flailed around for several seconds before going still. *He did it. It's over.*

Kate made her way around the mill. "Hey!" she shouted toward Chris, who turned around and looked at her. Sitting up, he gave a victorious hurrah with his fist in the air. In his hand, Chris was sporting a large knife. He was clearly injured, winded, and in need of assistance. She continued to walk toward Chris as she watched him slowly stand, wipe his face with his forearm, cough a few times, and dust off his knees. Surveying the situation, he peered back toward the barn. Glancing into the distance, Chris abruptly turned his gaze back to Kate in terror and screamed, "Run!" At that same moment, an arrow ripped through the air and struck him square in the neck.

Kate paused in horror as she watched Chris stand motionless for a few seconds and then collapse to the ground. She stood in frozen shock as a shadow emerged from around the barn and casually walked toward the farmhouse. It was a second assailant. He raised his hand and waved as he walked toward Chris. Kate struggled to clear her mind and assess the situation – the man had obviously spotted her but, for some reason, made no concerted effort to reload his weapon or run after her. She could tell the man was smiling. She looked down at Chris, who had just saved their lives; he now lay motionless in the dirt. Breaking her gaze, Kate turned and ran toward the mill.

"Run, little piggy, run," the unknown man behind her shouted as he laughed.

Kate quickly made it to the mill, rounded the corner, and grabbed Kevin by the shoulder and yanked. "We gotta go now."

"Wait, what happened?" Kevin began. "Where's Chris?"

"He's dead, and there's another guy out there."

Kevin looked at Kate in shock and didn't move.

"We move now or die," she said as she pulled him to the water. A few steps later, they both dove into the stream and swam for their lives.

28:45:11

M r. Black looked down at Chris, who was softly twitching as he continued to bleed out. The grass around his head was soaked in blood, and the color had drained from his skin. Looking down, Mr. Black made eye contact with Chris, whose head was turned to the side, away from the arrow. Mr. Black smiled and stood silently as the life faded from Chris.

He shifted his gaze a few feet over to the body of Mr. White, who lay face-up. Walking closer, Mr. Black crouched alongside the body and gazed at the large gash in Mr. White's neck; he had bled out in minutes. *Mortal wound on the first strike.* Mr. Black stood and shook his head in disgust, spitting on the ground next to Mr. White's body.

Across the field, a door clanked. Alert to his surroundings, Mr. Black quickly adjusted and drew an arrow. He took a deep breath and prepared to fire. To his surprise, a familiar face emerged and began marching toward him.

Not breaking eye contact with Mr. Black, Ranger made his way through the field toward the farmhouse.

"You missed all the fun," Mr. Black shouted.

"Oh, I saw everything just fine," he replied as he arrived at the bodies, standing a few feet from Mr. Black, who had lowered his weapon. "That was one hell of a shot."

"No, it wasn't," Mr. Black began as he looked down at Chris. "Kid gave me all day."

"That's probably because he was preoccupied," Ranger said as he gestured toward Mr. White's body.

"Isn't that the truth."

They both stared quietly at Mr. White's body. "The thing I don't get is, you were near the barn for several minutes before you fired. You saw everything unfold, and you clearly had an opportunity to assist Mr. White. Why didn't you?"

"I could say the same about you," Mr. Black responded while pointing the end of his bow toward the mill.

"I wouldn't have impacted the outcome from where I was, nor was I permitted to do so. But that's not the same for you."

Mr. Black paused and looked over at Mr. White's body. "Rules were crystal clear not to interfere with another man's pursuit."

"But when they were outside, he clearly wasn't faring well. You could have put an end to it."

"I could have," Mr. Black began, "but he sewed his fate."

"Please elaborate, if you don't mind." Ranger crossed his arms and glared at Mr. Black.

"He went into that house fully aware he was outnumbered. Closed quarters. Perfect for an ambush. He gave up his entire strategic advantage the second he stepped into the house. Whether it be arrogance, pride, or pure delusion that drove him in, his chances were slim to none from the get-go." Mr. Black paused and scratched his head. "Mark should have known better..."

"Mr. White," Ranger interrupted.

Mr. Black paused, smiled, and then walked closer to Ranger, who didn't move. "You can continue to play this naming game all you want. But you're not fooling anybody." Mr. Black turned and pointed at Mr. White. "That guy, right there, is Mark Wainwright, CEO of LTC. Pretty sure I have a stake in that company." Mr. Black paused. "And the other guy…"

"Mr. Blue," Ranger said, clearly not amused.

"Right, I don't remember his name off the top of my head, something Merrill. Doesn't matter, but I've seen his ass before as well on one of those finance shows. Fracking, I think, was the topic."

"And your point?"

"My point is, your contestants are prominent, well-known people. This cloak and dagger spy game makes no sense to me." Mr. Black shook his head.

Ranger paused and glared at Mr. Black, who was surprisingly on edge. "What about you?"

"What about me?" Mr. Black grunted.

"Who are you in all of this? You clearly have it all figured out; the odd man in this equation is you," Ranger added.

Smiling, Mr. Black swung his pack around his shoulder. "Me, I'm nobody."

"On that, we can agree."

Mr. Black looked back at Mr. White. "So, what happens next?"

"The Excursion Protocol. Standard operating procedure," Ranger said as he approached Mr. White's body and knelt. "Our friend here died in an unfortunate climbing accident."

"You got one of those fake stories for me?"

"You'll never know," Ranger said, looking up at Mr. Black. "Living men don't need one, dead men don't care."

Mr. Black smiled at Ranger. "You guys are worth every penny." He turned and began to walk toward the mill, waving his hand without looking back at Ranger.

Ranger stood and watched Mr. Black as he rounded the mill and followed the river's edge. Moments later, he disappeared from Ranger's line of sight. Ranger looked back down at the bodies and tapped his ear. "I need two bags, one white, one black. Let's execute Mr. White's

Excursion Protocol."

***

"Copy that," the Broker said while watching Ranger from the control room's main screen. "Will have two units to your location in a few minutes. We'll send them up through the mill gateway."

"Sounds good." Ranger paused and looked down again at the bodies. After a moment of silence, he continued, "I'd also like you to pull the file on Mr. Black for review."

"Confirmed. What are we looking for?" the Broker asked.

"I'm not sure yet, just one of those feelings."

"Understood." The Broker pivoted in his chair toward the tech to his right. "Refresh the board, please."

Scoreboard Update.
Mr. Black - 500 Points
Mr. Blue - 0 Points
Mr. White - 200 Points

28:11:16

They continued to kick and paddle as fast as their bodies could sustain. The current was far more manageable than upstream, but the depth was still a concern, as neither could touch bottom. Not letting Kevin out of her sight, Kate tried to hang a few feet back and shadow Kevin, just in case he needed her help. As she swam, she couldn't help but peer over her right shoulder from time to time. Though the farm had disappeared from her view some time ago, she was certain the pursuit was far from over. *I don't see anybody, but that doesn't mean we're not alone, not anymore.*

Slowing down to catch his breath, Kevin turned his body in the water toward Kate. "How much farther?"

"I'm not sure," she replied and slowed to meet him.

"Any idea where we are?"

"No," she said while breathing heavily and looking around. "But I think we should swim a bit more. Looks like the meadow ends just ahead. Once there's cover, we can go ashore."

"You're the boss," Kevin said as he turned and began to kick again.

The two continued downriver for another half hour before the tree line took form along the river; they occasionally paused to evaluate their surroundings and to catch their breaths. With the tree line in sight, Kevin let the current carry him and focused on keeping his head above water.

Kate spotted an opening along the bank of the river near the tree line and gestured Kevin to follow as she made her way to shore. They had to fight the current as they swam, but after a few minutes of kicking, they drew close to the edge. Eventually making bottom with her feet, Kate trudged through the water for the final few paces. Kevin followed closely.

Kate was the first to shore. She quickly turned and helped Kevin with his footing as he limped up the bank and took a seat along the first row of grass. Still standing, Kate surveyed the landscape. The river was in front of her and wound around to the left. To her right, the tree line broke, and the meadow opened up a few hundred feet away. To her six was dense forest, similar to the tree makeup from the far side of the meadow.

Staying calm and catching her breath, she turned back toward Kevin to examine his leg. Grabbing the cloth sleeves around his calf from the bottom, she pulled them down and revealed the wound. She evaluated the exit wound near his shin, and then rolled his leg a little and peered at the entry wound through his calf on the other side. "How's it feel?"

"It's felt worse," Kevin muttered. "At least I can put pressure on my leg now."

"Good," Kate replied. "You'll still need a doctor, and quite possibly some rehab, but you should pull through." Kate smirked.

Kevin rolled his eyes, drifted his head back, and took a deep breath.

Kate carefully repositioned the shirt sleeves over Kevin's leg. Silently sitting there, she continued to gaze at the sleeves long after they were set in position. *Chris.*

Rolling his head forward, Kevin reached out and gently placed his hand on her shoulder. "What happened back there?" He softly asked, breaking the silence.

Kate quickly broke her gaze and looked up at Kevin. "Huh?" she said in a bewildered daze.

"Back at the farm. You saw what happened, didn't you?"

How could I forget? Kate paused, looked down at the ground, and, after a deep breath, she shared with Kevin the events as they unfolded. The fight between Chris and the young man. How Chris killed him. The brief moment of elation. And finally, Chris' demise. "It all happened very fast."

"Did you get a look at the other guy?"

"For a second. He was older, heavier set, and he had the same bow as the other guy. I'm sure of that," Kate responded.

Kevin paused, contemplating his next words. "And you're sure Chris is gone?"

Sensing a bit of denial from Kevin and trying not to relive the moment in her head, Kate replied, "He took an arrow through the neck. He's gone, Kevin!"

"Sorry," Kevin said while holding his hand up. "I believe you, it's just crazy to think he's gone."

Kate knew Kevin was right. The events of the day had quickly escalated, far beyond anything she thought she would ever have to face or comprehend.

"How are you?" Kevin continued.

"Me? I'm fine," Kate said as she stood and began to pace.

"You saw two people die. Violently. I can only imagine how I'd react," Kevin said empathetically. "You even knew one of the people."

Kate locked in on Kevin. "Chris was my friend. You knew him too. And he saved us," she replied forcefully.

"He did," Kevin said softly, nodding.

"And you almost had me convinced," Kate said, now clearly irritated.

"Of what?"

"Oh, please. You've been skeptical of him since we got here."

"I had my suspicions." Kevin remained calm in response.

"Well, you were wrong, Kevin. He saved you, he saved both of us. He fixed your leg," she shouted while pointing at his calf. "And now he's gone. And Jesus, what about his family?"

Kate had known for some time that Chris' decision to delay entry into adulthood was not well-received by his family, especially his father, who came from a long line of white-collar executives and thought leaders in their respective fields. The truth was, Chris' decision ended in fallout, and he and his father hadn't spoken in several months. Chris had confided in Kate that he intended to make amends with his father in the coming months and start to look for a job. She knew he had always admired his father, especially because of his work ethic and rooted belief that a person should be judged only by what they did, and not where they came from. *Chris and his father would never have resolution.*

Kevin looked down at his leg. "You're right, I was wrong..."

"You need to get it together or we're not making it out of here. I need to be able to trust you, and right now I can't."

Kevin slowly stood, running his back along the trunk of a nearby tree. Kate moved forward to help, but Kevin gestured for her to stay. "You're right." Kevin grimaced as he rebalanced his weight. "I've been skeptical since the moment we got here, because none of this makes any sense, Kate. We were thrown into a field, with no gear, food, or water. Hours later, we're being shot at by some random guy with a bow," he said, flailing his arm in the air. "Now you're telling me there's a second." Kevin paused again. Kate remained silent. "Look, I didn't sign up for this..."

"Neither did I," Kate interrupted.

"And I'm scared. I'm not good at this stuff like you and Chris. I stand no chance out here," Kevin said while shifting his weight again. "I mean, look at me, I can barely move. I want to go home."

"I do too. And we will, if we stick together."

"How? We haven't even eaten all day, and I don't know about you, but I'm starving and have no clue how we're going to find food," Kevin continued.

Kate gazed in the direction of the farm. Overhead, the sun had started to shift west as it began its descent. Chris was gone, and she was now the best, and likely only, chance to survive. She took a deep breath and looked at Kevin. "Then let's start there," Kate said calmly.

"What?"

"Let's start with finding some food," she replied. "I don't know what all of this is either, but we're here, and we need to stick together if we're going to get out of this." She walked forward and embraced Kevin, which caught him completely off guard.

Standing back, Kate resurveyed their surroundings.

"So where do we start?" Kevin asked energetically. "Need me to make a spear or something?"

Kate smirked at the thought of Kevin building a hunting spear. "I think we should continue to those hills," she began while pointing up at the hillside to the west. "We should stick close to the water, which might also give us a few options to eat."

"What are we going to eat?"

"Oh, you'll see." Kate rolled her eyes and began to walk west near the edge of the river. Kevin pivoted and began to follow.

26:25:57

Near the base of the western hills, the river took a sharp turn to the south. At the bend, there were several downed, moss-ridden trees along the riverside. Kate carefully walked between the trees and, keeping her gaze down, occasionally kicked the trunks with her boot and then moved on. Several trees later, Kate knelt in front of one. She waved for Kevin to come over. Eager to see what Kate was doing, Kevin quickly hobbled toward where she knelt.

"We should have a few options here," Kate said as she stood next to the trunk.

"Where?"

In a swift lunge, Kate drove her foot into the trunk, which quickly crumbled. Kate knelt and began to pull away the rotting wood. Reaching in, she ran her hand along the inside of the tree, which, to Kevin's surprise, had hollow spots. Kate paused in her search, looked up at Kevin, and smiled as she quickly removed her hand from the tree, revealing several white, elongated objects in her hand.

"What the hell are those?" Kevin said with disgust.

"Dinner," Kate replied. "Wood-boring beetle larva, I believe. I've had them a few times and they're actually not bad." Reaching down with her left hand, Kate plucked one of the white objects, dropped it in her mouth, and began to chew.

"I'm not touching those."

"Suit yourself," Kate replied as she ate another. "They're actually rich in protein."

"What happened to hunting or fishing?" Kevin said while haphazardly turning and looking around at the ground and into the woods.

Kate ate a third. "There's next to zero chance we could catch an animal, if that's what you're suggesting. First, we'd have to figure out a mechanism to catch and kill something, which could take hours. Second, we'd actually have to hunt, which is equally time intensive. And after all that, there's no guarantee we'd catch anything," Kate concluded.

"What about fishing?"

"Sure, fashion a spear and go stand out there. Have you ever done it before?"

"No."

"Didn't think so. Also, not a good use of our time and efforts. Plus, you'd be completely exposed standing out at the river."

Kate had a point. "So, this is our only option?" Kevin asked while returning his attention to the white objects in Kate's hand.

"I'm sure there are some grubs beneath some of these trees if you'd like to give those a try." Kate smirked. "Look, we've been going all day. Our bodies are depleted. The sun will be gone in a few hours, and someone wants us dead. We need to load up where and when we can." Kate gestured forward and held out a larva for Kevin.

Kevin hesitated. "Can't we at least cook these?"

"And send up a signal to that other guy that we're right here? Not a chance."

"Yeah, that didn't work out well last time," Kevin said as he thought back to the events at the farmhouse.

Kate understood his reference and didn't want to revisit those memories. She shoved the larva in his face. "Take it or starve. It's your call."

Rolling his eyes, Kevin reached down and took the larva from her hand. He looked at it closely, giving it a sniff as well.

"Oh. just eat it," Kate said as she returned to the trunk to gather more food.

Closing his eyes, Kevin dropped the larva in his mouth and began to chew. *Dammit, these actually aren't that bad. I'm never admitting that to her.*

25:10:07

"We have a decision to make," Kate began as she and Kevin wrapped up their meal. "The river bend heads south, but the field where we saw that helicopter is to the north."

"What's our best chance of getting out of here?" Kevin asked.

"I'm honestly not sure. Sticking close to water makes a lot of sense, and maybe it'll lead us out of here," Kate said as she shifted her gaze north, "but we clearly saw some activity that way."

"And we don't know what it is," Kevin continued. "We don't know if there's water, and that other guy from the farm is over there somewhere..."

"Presumably."

Kevin looked straight ahead at the hillside across from the river. "Why don't we go up the hill right here and scope things out? You said it yourself earlier that the sun will disappear behind those hills in a little while," Kevin continued. "We could climb up, maybe preserve some sunlight in the process, and get a better sense for where to go next from up top."

"And water?"

"Maybe there are springs like the other hills. If not, we know this river is here and we can double back."

Kate stood, dusting off her knees, and looked up at the hill. Kevin's points were valid. "We'll need to cross the river again."

"That's OK. The water feels good on my leg," Kevin responded while gesturing down at his wound.

They crossed the river with relative ease. The current had dissipated even farther from where they had previously come onshore some miles back. Kate was able to reach the bottom across the entirety of the crossing, which allowed for her to more easily assist Kevin. Making quick work of the opposite riverbank, Kate and Kevin exited the river and immediately started making their way through the tree-covered incline and up the hill.

Kevin took extra precautions during the ascent to watch his footing and avoid rubbing up against any trees. Though weak, he was making good on only asking Kate for assistance in a few instances, mostly when having to climb over protruding boulders and stone faces. Different from their previous climb, Kate had let Kevin lead the way, which he relished.

"Need a break?" Kate asked as she looked down at her watch. "We started at the river around 25:10 on the countdown, so we've been at this for nearly thirty minutes."

"I'm good," Kevin responded. "Unless you're looking for a break?"

"Maybe in a few. Wouldn't hurt to start keeping our eyes peeled for a good place to rest." Kate knew they had to keep pace. They were starting to run short on sunlight, and they needed to get as high as they could. She also knew not to push too hard on the ascent. *He's still out there, and we need to save our strength, especially if we have to make a sudden break for cover. We're also not going to make it much farther; our pace is too slow.*

"What do you think that is?" Kevin said as he paused the hike and pointed forward.

Kate arrived at his side and peered toward where he was pointing. A few rows of trees in front of them, a brown object leaning against a tree. "Is that a shovel?"

"Let's find out," Kevin said as he moved forward.

Approaching the object, Kate sped up and went around Kevin. Leaning against a nearby tree was an old shovel. The handle was a rusted metal loop, the shaft made of faded wood, and the end was flat, approximately ten inches long and eight inches wide. Kate reached forward and picked it up.

"Looks old as hell," Kevin said as he arrived at Kate's side.

"Yeah, the metal is heavy, but there actually isn't much corrosion," she replied as she inspected the shovel. "This might be useful." She stood and handed the shovel to Kevin. "It'll help with the climb; use it as a crutch or walking stick."

"Thanks."

Kate turned and began to lead the way up the hill. A few short paces later, she immediately paused and crouched down to her knees. Raising her hand to shield her line of sight, she peered up the hill. Turning to Kevin, she began to smile. "Think I know where that came from," Kate said as she gestured toward the shovel. "This way."

Straight ahead, the forest quickly opened up to reveal a small man-made establishment. A pile of logs was leaning against the edge, using existing trees to keep them in place. Straight ahead was a small wooden shed with windows on all sides. The terrain was mostly flat dirt, with a light mix of weeds and forest growth covering the surface; the clearing was definitely man-made. Twenty meters ahead, the slope of the hill aggressively rose, creating a small cliff before the hill resumed. Right against the incline was another wooden structure nestled against a stone surface.

Kate and Kevin slowly edged out from the trees and into the opening. Neither said a word as they cautiously surveyed the location. Kate turned to Kevin and gestured for him to follow her. Turning toward the shed, she carefully made her way across the clearing, landing softly with each step.

Kate arrived at the shed on the right side and peered inside. The nearby window was at her shoulder level, small, and chalky from years of environmental buildup. She couldn't make out what was inside. Kate pushed back and wrapped around to the front of the shed toward the door. Kevin arrived by Kate's side as she approached. Across the front of the entrance was an old sliding locking mechanism.

"Think it'll open?" Kevin asked.

"Let's find out," Kate replied as she reached forward, grabbed the U-shaped bend in the metal. She forcefully shimmied the metal bend from a downward to upward-facing position. With a tug, she heaved to the right. The door released. Letting go of the rusted metal lock, she wiped her hands on the side, reached for the door handle, and pulled. The door creaked open.

Kate and Kevin peered inside. The room was empty. Made of wood, the interior was covered with dust, highlighted from the rays of sunshine coming through the chalky windows. On the walls were large rusted nails protruding from the weight-bearing supports, clearly used as hooks. Kate slowly walked in, coughing as she inhaled the dust, and inspected the floor.

"See here," she said, pointing toward the floor, "there are differences in level the of dust all over."

Kevin hobbled in, looked down, and was able to make out what she was showing. "What does that mean?"

"It means this shed was cleared out, and from the buildup, not too long ago," she replied as she glanced up at the ceiling and around the structure, looking for anything that could be foraged.

"At least we have some shelter."

"That we do," Kate said as she wrapped her inspection and walked slowly back to the door. "For the second time today."

"Where are you going?" Kevin asked as he turned to follow.

"I want to check out that other structure just over there," Kate replied as she gestured behind Kevin's left shoulder.

"Any idea what it is?"

"I think this might be a mining camp of some sort..."

"You think that's a mine?" Kevin interrupted.

"Yes, and I'm hoping they left something else behind," Kate added while gesturing toward the shovel Kevin was still holding.

"Works for me," Kevin said as he passed by Kate and made his way to the entrance of the shed. Kate followed closely behind.

With a ripping thud, an arrow drove into the door frame just above Kevin's right shoulder.

"Get down!" Kate screamed as she surged forward, pushing Kevin through the door and diving around the right corner of the shed. The scramble occurred in a few seconds, and Kate had them both on the far-right side wall.

Kevin fell on his back as Kate pivoted to the shed's edge and tried to slow her breathing. "Did you see where it came from?" Kevin said as he began to stand.

Kate snapped her arm and gestured for him to stay tight to the shed.

"Kate?"

"Kitty-corner from where we're standing," she replied while nodding over her left shoulder. "Near where we came up." Taking a deep breath, she quickly peered around the edge and attempted to survey the site. *Nothing.* Kate shifted her head back to the cover of the shed.

"See anything?" Kevin asked, leaning against the shed right next to Kate.

"No," she whispered. *But he's out there.*

"What do we do?"

Kate looked at the tree line to her left and in front of where she stood. Then to the sharp incline to her right. *No way we make it to the trees.* Kate softly pushed off from the shed and headed toward the back corner, carefully making her way around Kevin, who flipped his head and shimmied after her.

She looked along the sharp incline of the cutaway hill. *Not much better on this side.* Surveying from right to left, her eyes landed on the second structure, which she was now positive was a mine entrance. She examined its exterior for a few more seconds; it was overall unremarkable and resembled the build of the shed, with a door in front, and the roof came to a point.

"Alright, you're not going to like this," she began, "but we're going to run for that second structure over there." Kate pointed toward the mine entrance.

"Why not head toward the trees back there?" Kevin replied while turning his head to the left.

"He's over there somewhere," she replied. "I couldn't find him, but he's in those trees, and I guaranteed he'll pick us off. Plus, the only way we can run in that direction is downhill, which means we give up the high ground, and again, he picks us off."

Kevin looked back at Kate, who peered around the corner once more, and then turned back. "The other structure is probably forty, maybe fifty feet away. If we run, it might throw him off just long enough for us to get inside."

"And if we get inside, then what?"

"Then we figure out our next move."

"I'm not sure I agree with this plan. If we somehow make it over there alive, and if we get inside, we'll be trapped."

Kate looked sternly at Kevin. "Your only alternative is to stay right here, and I promise you, if this guy is even remotely intelligent, he's working on flanking us right now."

Kevin swung his head toward the tree line and examined the perimeter. No movement, but she's right. He looked back at Kate and nodded.

"Now give me that," she said, gesturing toward the shovel. "Once we round the corner, run as fast as you can. I'm going to run ahead and get the door free." She turned and inched around the corner. Quickly turning back, she motioned for Kevin to stay close. "You got this. Keep low and keep moving; don't make yourself an easy target."

In a sudden burst, Kate took off for the shed. Kevin hobbled behind her, but to his surprise, and thanks to a surge in adrenaline, he was able to keep reasonably close. *Just ten more steps. Kate is almost there.*

Kate arrived at the structure, and, unable to slow in time, she slammed into the wood panels along the side. Still grasping the shovel, she shifted to the door and pulled. The door was locked. Looking down, she found the door was secured by a shiny, modern padlock. "You've got to be shitting me."

Kevin arrived at the shed just as an arrow struck the door inches from Kate's face. Kevin looked up, astonished at Kate's fortune. *Did he just miss, or is he playing with us?*

Looking at the door's handles, Kate turned the shovel in hand and hammered it down on them twice. The metal loosened. Giving the handles a tug, a nail released, and the door was ajar. Kate quickly swung it open, and she and Kevin dove into the dark interior.

***

The Broker leaned forward in his chair and glared intently at the main screen. Leaning back, he adjusted his glasses and peered left. "Please tell me we cleaned out that mine and didn't just haphazardly set a padlock and call it a day."

Nobody responded.

25:03:33

The large wooden door made a loud creak as Kate pulled it shut. Small beams of sun shone through the cracks between the boards. Turning back to Kevin, she knew they didn't have much time. Their gamble had paid off, at least temporarily. Looking forward, Kate peered down the long winding tunnel of an old mine shaft. Large wooden trusses ran up the side of the walls and over the ceiling of the tunnel every ten feet. The air was humid and musty.

"Keep going," Kate said as she gestured for Kevin to go deeper into the tunnel. Looking back at the door, she knew their light would run short quickly, and the last thing they wanted was to venture through an old mine shaft with no light. "Look for something to burn." She gestured to Kevin as she walked over to the edge of the tunnel and began to search for anything left behind.

"How the hell did we just survive that?" Kevin asked as he struggled to catch his breath.

"I don't know," she responded quietly. "Keep looking." *We shouldn't be alive if that was the same person who shot Chris at distance.*

"What about this?" Kevin said from the other side of the tunnel, as he stood next to an old wooden table with a cloth draped over the top.

"Perfect," she said as she darted over to Kevin's side. Kevin pulled the cloth to his side, revealing the surface of an old workstation. "Help me with this," Kate said as she moved to the table's edge and began to flip it onto its side. Kevin quickly moved to the other corner of the table and began to push. Seconds later they had the table on its side.

"Okay, I need you to rip off a piece from that cloth—decent size," Kate said as she quickly made her way back to the entrance where she had dropped the rusted shovel. Moments later she was back at the table with the shovel in hand. Quickly surveying the table, she took the large end of the shovel, drove it between two of the boards, and began to pull. As she moved the shovel back and forth, a sideboard began to creak and loosen. "Watch out," she grunted, still pulling on the loose board. In a sudden snap, the board flung loose. Kate set the shovel down, braced her foot, and, with a series of tugs, removed the loosened board from the table.

Kate walked around the table and crouched down next to Kevin, who had taken a seat and was tearing away a piece of fabric from the sheet. "Is this big enough?" he asked while gesturing to a piece roughly three feet long and ten inches wide.

"Perfect, make a few more," Kate replied as she gestured for Kevin to hand her the fabric. Looking back at the door, Kate knew they would likely have a visitor at any moment. *We need to keep moving. We need to move faster.* Kate quickly wrapped the fabric around the end of the piece of pried wood. Reaching to her pocket, she pulled out the book of matches. Kate dropped the wood between her legs and held it upright with her thighs. Quickly removing a match from the matchbook, she struck the tip. A small flame erupted as she gently brought her hand down to the fabric. As she held the burning match along the material, it began to catch. Kate withdrew the match and waved it out. Reaching down, she grabbed another match and struck it. Bringing the second match to the other side of the cloth, she started a second fire. Seconds later the flames took off, converged, and engulfed the end of the board.

"Nice," Kevin said as he stood, holding two pieces of torn fabric.

"Good to go?" Kate asked while smiling up at the flame.

Kevin nodded.

"Alright, make sure you bring all of that cloth with you. Let's go," she said while looking back once more at the tunnel entrance, still undisturbed. "And watch your step; who knows what we'll find in here."

Kate and Kevin slowly made their way deeper into the tunnel. The makeshift torch provided sufficient light to navigate their surroundings, but Kate wasn't sure how long their fabric supply would last and was reluctant to go too deep into the mineshaft. "Keep your eyes peeled," she said, looking down at her feet, and then paused. "Actually, take a look over there," she continued while pointing to the left side of the tunnel, "and I'll stay over here." Kate pointed to the right side of the tunnel. Kevin nodded and shifted over to the opposite side of the tunnel.

Step by step, they drove deeper into the tunnel. Looking back, Kate could still make out the entrance. *What is he waiting for?* The tunnel was mostly empty. Aside from the table they found near the entrance, the only thing either had spotted since was a rusted bucket, which Kevin confirmed had nothing inside.

Continuing forward, Kate spotted an inlet along the right side of the tunnel. Moving quickly forward, she came to its edge and peered inside. The pocket stretched from one wooden strut to the next, approximately ten feet, and only a few feet deep. As she canvased the inlet, an object on the ground caught her eye—a wooden box. The box was made of dark wood with black inscriptions on the long side facing Kate. She knelt for a closer look. The text was obfuscated by a white crust that appeared to seep between the boards. "Check this out," Kate said to Kevin as she leaned closer to the box. "I wonder what's inside."

Kevin peered across the tunnel. "Holy shit." Kevin lunged across the tunnel toward Kate, and in a sudden jerk grabbed her arm and pulled her away from the box and onto her rear. "No!" he shouted, while trying to catch his breath.

"What the hell, Kevin..."

"Don't touch that," Kevin implored as he knelt and inspected the box from a distance. "And keep that torch away." Leaning in, Kevin peered around all edges of the box, took a deep breath, and then sat back next to Kate.

"What's in the box...?" Kate halted as her attention diverted to the sound of a creak coming from the front of the tunnel. "He's here," Kate whispered to Kevin.

Looking back at the entrance, Kevin got to his feet, reached over, and offered Kate his hand. "Do you trust me?"

"Do I have a choice?"

24:46:51

Pulling the large wooden door open with a loud creak, Mr. Black cautiously entered the mine. He had elected to hydrate for several minutes and give the prey a better opportunity to hide before continuing the pursuit. Stepping inside, he was struck with the musty and humid whiff of the tunnel's interior. Pausing near the entrance, he surveyed his immediate surroundings, bow in hand. The mine shaft quickly turned dark, and aside from a broken table to his right, there wasn't much in terms of debris or hazardous materials that he could see.

"Knock knock," he shouted down the tunnel, "anybody home?"

There was no response.

Mr. Black smirked and began his slow march into the darkness of the tunnel beyond. He gazed around at the tunnel's design. The shaft was well-constructed, but easily over a hundred years old; he found no sign of cables or electricity along the surfaces, and the wood supporting the structure had clearly come from the trees in the surrounding area.

Something about the tunnel and the chase at hand brought him back to his childhood in the foothills of Pennsylvania. Mr. Black grew up an only child in an affluent family. His father, a managing partner of a law firm in Philadelphia, was rarely around, and his mother was often preoccupied by nine a.m. with her morning bottle of Heidsieck. He shared little love or admiration for either of his parents and spent the majority of his youth moving in and out of private schools across the state. It was in his early teenage years that he began to appreciate the thrills of outdoor excursions and began to refine his hunting skills on local house pets. But after being caught in the act one summer by a neighboring groundskeeper, he shifted his attention to bigger game. He was a mere fifteen years old when he took down his first black bear, and it wasn't long after that his attention shifted away from the Northeast and toward more exotic and challenging locations. Alaska. Panama. Brazil. Uganda.

Mr. Black's parents had died suddenly in a car accident while he was out on excursion, around the time of his eighteenth birthday. Overnight, he inherited the masses of his family's wealth. Not overly eager to continue the family business, Mr. Black instead spent the majority of his adult life devoted to travel and acquisition of historic and collectible texts. He knew early on the importance of perpetuating his estate and diversified his assets across the globe. He had a unique eye for emerging tech. In the years that followed, his passion for hunting and outdoor excursions dissipated and was replaced entirely by his business interests and an overzealous gambling addiction.

It was by pure coincidence that he had learned of APEX. Mr. Black had found himself invited to an exclusive poker game at an undisclosed location in Rio. The participants were the familiar mix of ambitious youths with access to the deep pockets of their parents, and the public aristocrats seeking a night of thrill. It was at the table that an older man had politely inquired as to why Mr. Black was in Rio. Understanding the rules of etiquette at such events, Mr. Black obliged him with a tale of his Amazonian hunt, none of which was true, as he preferred to keep his business dealings close to the chest. They shared pleasantries over the course of several drinks, and it was in the man's departing words that he said, "I'll see to it we get you on the list." Mr. Black had no clue what the drunken man had meant, until his phone rang some days later.

And here I am.

Continuing his slow trek down the tunnel, Mr. Black caught a glimpse of a shadow to his right. Cautiously moving to his left, he set his bow on target. He carefully inched toward the shadow. Several steps later, he was able to clearly make out the shadow; it was Kevin.

"Giving up so easily?" Mr. Black smirked. "I must admit, I was hoping for a bit of a chase, though I'm guessing from the state of your leg that it wouldn't be too much fun." Mr. Black gestured the arrowhead down toward Kevin's wounded leg.

Kevin stood motionless and didn't respond.

"And where's your little friend?" Mr. Black continued. "Bet she's around here somewhere."

"I'm here alright," a voice responded near Kevin, out of sight.

Curious, Mr. Black shifted to his left and was able to make out the second target. They were both standing in a small alcove; she was just off his left hip, standing slightly behind him. "There you are, sweetheart." Mr. Black smiled. "Any chance I could persuade the two of you to join me outside?"

"We'll take our chances in here, instead of being picked off out there," Kevin replied.

"Oh, 'picked off' isn't how I'd put it at all."

"Tell that to Chris," Kate replied.

"Ahh, your friend at the farm," Mr. Black began. "I have to hand it to him, he put up a good fight against Mr. White. To his credit, that was one hell of a strike with the knife."

"You murdered him," Kevin added.

"As I recall, your friend murdered one of my fellow compatriots. He played by his rules, and I played by mine." Mr. Black took his bow and pointed it at Kevin. "Though I suppose by that notion, we should just get on with things then, eh?"

"We should," Kevin began, "and let's start by changing up the rules."

Kevin quickly spread his legs, revealing a wooden box between them.

Mr. Black paused and gestured toward the box with his arrow. "Now what do you have there?"

"A little souvenir left from the miners."

Mr. Black glared down at the box. *Dynamite.* Quickly looking up at Kate and Kevin, he took a deep breath. In a swift motion, he aimed and fired his bow at the torch in Kate's hand. The arrow quickly struck the shaft of the torch and drove it from Kate's hand to the ground, away from the box.

"You were saying?" Mr. Black said as he pulled another arrow from his pack. "Not sure how you plan to set off dynamite without a fire source, and that's also assuming those sticks have firing caps that still work."

Kevin nodded. "All very true."

Mr. Black smiled and placed the arrow into position and aimed at Kevin.

"But you see, there's still a problem," Kevin continued. "It's quite humid in here, wouldn't you say?"

"Yes, indeed," Mr. Black said, trying to figure out Kevin's angle. *Is he stalling?*

"See those white spots on the box? That means these sticks have been sweating, and for quite some time. Humidity and old dynamite don't get along well."

Mr. Black suddenly realized what Kevin was saying. He took a step back. "Nitro?"

Kevin smiled and nodded. "This box is highly unstable. You shoot either of us, we fall, and this thing goes off. And there's plenty in here to bring this place down, and that's only of concern if you somehow survive the initial blast."

Scratching his head, Mr. Black hesitated. Quickly looking around the tunnel, he realized the prey had turned his advantage around. That was, if the box actually went off with somebody falling on it. *But am I willing to take that risk?* He peered down at the box again, the white crust now more obvious than before.

Stepping back, Mr. Black looked at the door to the tunnel and then lowered the arrow. "I have to admit," Mr. Black said, "very well played, you two. Though I'm not sure you thought this one all the way through. I'm clearly not going to surrender. I'd rather set that box off myself than capitulate to either of you. Which means your only play is to drive me out of here, which is fine. But then what?"

Kevin looked over at Kate.

"'Cause, you see," Mr. Black continued, "there's only one way out of here, and that's where I'll be." He pointed toward the door, turned, and began to walk. "I admire what you did right here, real survival instinct. Because of that, I'm going to give you the night to think it over. If, by tomorrow morning, you remain reluctant to join me outside, I will detonate that box, and if you think I can't hit that from outside, think again."

Mr. Black smiled and headed toward the exit.

24:30:12

"Well, that didn't go quite as planned," Kate said to Kevin as she watched Mr. Black exit and close the door behind him.

"How do you figure?" Kevin replied.

"We're in the same situation we were a half-hour ago, but now we have that." Kate gestured toward the box at Kevin's feet. "And now he knows it's there." Kate pushed off from the cove and walked into the main tunnel, rubbing her forehead. "Don't get me wrong, that was really slick what you did there, but to what end?"

Kevin stepped away from the box and joined Kate. "You've missed the most important part: we now have time."

"Assuming he actually stays out there all night and doesn't attempt to kill us in our sleep," Kate interrupted.

"Right, but let's assume he stays out there. We have now, what? Ten hours?"

Kate stopped and looked at Kevin, who clearly had more to his plan.

"There's something about this tunnel that's been bothering me," Kevin continued. "The humidity, where's it coming from?"

"You think there's something deeper in the tunnel?"

"Maybe," Kevin replied. "Either way, that man with the bow just gave us ample time to figure out what else is in here."

"So, we're going deeper into the mine?"

"Yes, we are."

Recovering their shovel and striking a new flame to the torch, Kate and Kevin descended deeper into the mine. The tunnel turned a sharp left shortly after the cove and angled to a steep decline. Using the walls, Kate and Kevin trudged down into the darkness. Their steps echoed off the walls and pierced the silence of the tunnel. Descending deeper, Kate and Kevin didn't initially find any remnants of the miners, though they did come across a second alcove with a small wooden shelving unit inside. Quickly inspecting the shelves, Kevin didn't spot anything useful.

Turning another corner, this time to the right, the tunnel leveled off. "How far down do you think we've gone?" Kevin asked.

"Not sure, easily two hundred feet, if not more." Kate continued to forge forward with the torch in hand. Kevin had quietly shifted back to using the shovel as a crutch.

"That's about what I was thinking too; I wonder how far this thing goes?"

Continuing down the mine shaft, Kevin and Kate came upon an opening. The tunnel abruptly opened into a large working station. The ceiling nearly doubled in height, though still suspended by the same wooden framework, and the room extended several paces to the left and right. The place had clearly housed mining equipment at some point, but aside from a few metal rail pieces stacked against the wall, it was now empty.

In the distance, a sliding sound echoed through the tunnel. The sound was similar to two pieces of wood rubbing together. "You hear that?"

Standing silently, Kevin listened. *Slide. Slide.* "Yup." He paused and listened again. "And I think I know what it is." Gesturing for Kate to follow, he took off down the tunnel.

Several paces later, Kevin slowed his rate and then abruptly halted and looked down. Kate did the same. In front of them was a rusted metal rowboat. Kate raised the torch higher and waved it around the boat. It was sitting in water.

"The hell?" she said. *What is a boat doing several hundred feet underground?*

"It's an underground river," Kevin said. "I bet this is why there's not much in this mine. They hit water, realized they couldn't dig further, and pulled out."

"I think we need to see where this goes," Kate added.

"Absolutely," Kevin replied. "Can you stabilize the boat while I step in?" Kate nodded and made her way over to the boat, knelt, and held it against the edge. Kevin slowly stepped in, scanned for leaks, and took a seat. Handing Kevin the torch, then the shovel, Kate carefully slid in the boat and had a seat opposite Kevin. "We were due for some good luck," Kevin said as he wrapped a new piece of cloth around the burning board and gestured to Kate for the matches. Moments later, Kevin had the fire renewed, handed Kate the torch, carefully placed the shovel over the side of the boat, and began to row.

***

Taking turns rowing, they slowly made their way deeper into the abyss. The river remained mostly straight, though there were a few instances where Kate and Kevin had to duck into the boat to clear the cave ceiling. Luckily, those sections were short-lived, and Kate and Kevin were able to sit comfortably. The initial fire Kevin lit before they set out had only lasted twenty minutes at most, by Kate's estimation. She quickly reset the torch with a fresh swath of cloth from Kevin. Onward they rowed. The stream was silent, as if they were the first to disturb the surface in generations, and in all likelihood, that was probably the case.

The cave remained humid, and small droplets of water fell from the ceiling and dripped softly down to the water's surface and into the boat.

The drops echoed through the cave as they both tried to listen for any unnatural sounds. Kate moved the torch around the front perimeter of the boat to constantly survey their surroundings. There were clusters of small stalagmites along the edge of the water to the left, followed by a rigid stone wall that rose over their heads.

In a sudden jolt, the boat ground to a halt. It came as a surprise to Kevin and Kate, and they both shifted forward to see a large rock wall just below the surface blocking their path. Kate handed Kevin the torch, inched toward the front of the boat, put her hands on the rock, and pushed. The boat drifted slightly backward. "Give me that," Kate said to Kevin, gesturing for the flame. Glaring forward, the tunnel quickly came to an end. Raising the torch over her head and to her left and right, she came to the realization their trip might be over. *Dead end.*

"What should we do now?" Kevin asked.

"We can't head back," Kate muttered. "Dammit, I really thought we had this one." She leaned over and splashed the water in frustration.

"Maybe we missed a turn or something. If we head back..."

"No," Kate interrupted softly as she gazed into the water that she'd just disturbed.

Realizing Kate was staring at something, Kevin leaned forward. "What is it?"

"Hold this," Kate said, handing Kevin the torch. Rolling forward, she dropped into the water. "Be right back." Kate submerged and disappeared.

Kevin sat silently in the boat, peering over the side, nervously looking for Kate. Several seconds later, she surfaced and grabbed the edge of the boat but made no attempt to get in as she coughed and caught her breath.

"What's going on?" Kevin asked.

"I saw light down there." She smiled. "There's a cave, and it opens up on the other side."

"What's in there?"

"Not sure yet, just went down to see if I could make it."

"And?"

"Won't be easy; the cave is at least fifteen, maybe twenty feet long, but I think we can get to the bottom and then swim up on the other side."

Kevin stared apprehensively at Kate.

"Don't worry, you can go first," she added. "I'll drown well before you."

Kevin smirked and slowly rounded the edge of the boat and got in the water. "There's no going back, is there?"

"Nope." Kate smiled.

The water was surprisingly warm. Grabbing the side of the boat, Kevin made his way over to Kate.

"Deep breath on three. You head straight down along the wall, and the cave opens up about twelve feet down, then through the cave."

"Then what?"

"Then we hope there's an opening. Otherwise that guy with the bow is going to be extremely disappointed."

Kevin nodded.

"One, two, three." Both took a deep breath and submerged. Kate watched as Kevin kicked his way to the rock wall and down to the entrance of the cave. At the opening, he stopped and looked inside. Kate caught up and gestured for him to go. Kevin shook his head as he continued to shift his arms and keep his body in position. With her lungs starting to burn, Kate grabbed Kevin by the shoulder and shoved him forward.

Swimming as hard as she could, she followed Kevin through the cave. *This is a lot longer than I thought.* Lungs burning and a headache mounting, Kate closed her eyes and continued to kick. She felt the energy drain from her body. She knew they were running out of time and still had half of the cave to go. She closed her eyes and continued to kick and claw.

Her body began to tremble and spasm. In a reflexive motion, she lifted her head and smacked it into the stone slate above. Not having time to react, she kept kicking. *This was a terrible idea. This is probably it.* Moments later, her head jolted up again, though this time nothing happened. Kate quickly opened her eyes and looked up. *I'm clear.* Shifting her body vertical and kicking with every ounce of life she had left, she thrust upward.

Kate burst through the surface of the water, gasping for air as she choked and fought to keep upright. She was dizzy and seeing stars but could tell there was still daylight, though it had fallen behind the hills for the day. Continuing to kick and squirm, she spit out another mouthful of water. *I shouldn't be alive; how many more second chances am I going to get?*

Looking up at the sky, she began to calm her breathing. Elated to still be alive, she let out a deep breath and began to look around. "Kevin?" she coughed, while spitting out more water.

Quickly swiveling around on the surface, she began to breathe more heavily. The adrenaline from her near-death experience was briefly contained and then reignited at the thought of losing Kevin. With each new breath, her vision improved. Continuing to swivel around in the water, she looked for any sign of Kevin.

Moments later, she caught the sound of another person hacking and splashing in the water. Shifting around, she spotted Kevin flailing on the surface about thirty feet away. Adjusting her position, she started to swim his direction.

Kevin quickly spotted Kate. "We did it." He laughed while coughing erratically. Kate arrived at his side seconds later with a trickle of blood running down her face. "Holy shit, are you okay?"

Kate raised her hand to the spot where she had smacked into the rocks. She was bleeding. Rinsing the blood off her hand in the water, she shrugged. "All things considered, I'll be alright."

"I don't remember seeing this from the hills, do you?" Kevin asked.

Kate examined their surroundings; they were in a small lake at the base of a giant hill. "Nope, but I think that's where we just came from," she replied while pointing toward a mountainous hill rising ahead. "Let's go," she added as she started to kick toward the shore.

"Wait, can't we pause for a minute and reflect on what just happened?" Kevin asked. "Look at what we just survived."

"I have," Kate replied as she continued to drift toward the shore, "and I'd like to stay alive a bit longer."

22:10:11

K evin had never been more relieved to be on land and above ground. Coming out of the water, he stumbled to the closest tree, still breathing heavily, fell to his knees, and hugged the trunk. Kate followed closely behind, though she made no effort to embrace the environment as Kevin did. The hill stood in front of them, the lake at their backs, and Kate was able to make out the fading sunlight as it shone on the ridge to the east, now farther away than before.

"I think we're south of the mine," she began. "I bet you if we go up here, but stay to the left, we can come out right on top of the rock face that surrounded the mining area." Kate pointed up the hill.

Kevin looked up at Kate and shook his head. "I'm not going anywhere near that place, ever again."

"How else do you presume we get out of here? The plan hasn't changed; we need to get to the top of that hill and see what's going on."

"And get shot in the process," Kevin barked.

"It's a risk to head back up there, but it's a risk anywhere we go. At least in this scenario, we'll have the advantage."

Kevin blinked and Kate and shook his head. "I don't follow."

"Assuming that guy stays true to his word, we know exactly where he'll be," Kate continued. "We can keep clear of where he should be, and maybe even get some rest."

"Until he finds us," Kevin muttered while shaking his head.

"I don't think he will."

"And what makes you think that? How many times does he need to shoot at you before you change your mind?"

"The mine. He thinks we're still trapped inside," Kate said while pointing to the eastern side of the hill where the mine was located, now clearly frustrated. "He's not going to be looking for us. Hell, he might even sleep himself."

Kevin began to pace between the trees. He looked up at the fading sun and knew the light would soon be gone.

"It's risky, but it's even riskier to stay here," she added. "He's not going to leave that site."

Kevin turned and raised his finger. "If I agree to this, and that's a big if, I want you to promise me that at any time, I can end this. If even for one second I don't think this is a good idea and want to change course, we will."

"Within reason," Kate replied with a smile as she offered her fist. Kate knew fully well that this was the only way she would get Kevin where she knew they needed to go.

Kevin hesitated and then bumped his fist with hers.

The sunlight was nearly gone by the time they got started. Luckily, it was a clear night and the moon lit the sky and sent rays through the treetops down to the forest floor. The sound of insects owned the night, a sound Kevin had become increasingly accustomed to. Leading the way up the hill, Kate made a concerted effort to watch how much noise they were making; each step was carefully marked, and Kevin followed her with as much precision as his leg would allow.

Both remained silent during the climb. Occasionally stopping during the ascent, Kate would turn to Kevin and make sure he was holding up. In all of the chaos of the previous few hours, she tried to not forget that earlier in the day, he had been impaled by an arrow. She admired his drive to keep moving and couldn't remember the last time he had complained about his leg.

Coming up a sharp ridge, Kate paused at the smell of smoke. Closing in behind, Kevin sensed it as well. They both crouched down. Kate turned back to Kevin. "We're close; I think that incline in front of us might be the side of the mine area," Kate whispered as she pointed straight forward and slightly to the right.

"Right, so let's go to the left." Kevin pointed as well.

"I think we should take a look," she responded.

"What good would that do except to give him an opportunity to spot us?"

Kate shrugged. "Maybe he's asleep. And if so, maybe we can sneak in and get his gear, or possibly even his weapons."

Kevin shook his head. "That's the dumbest thing I've heard from you all day, Kate."

Kate looked back in the direction where the smoke was coming from. After a moment, she turned to Kevin, smiled, and started making her way up the hill to the right.

"Kate," Kevin whispered as he began to follow her, "you promised."

Pausing, Kate turned around. "You are more than welcome to head the other way, but I'm going to scope this guy out. Is it a risk? By every conventional standard, yes." She paused. "But nothing about this is normal. Normal rules have gone out the window. Chris is dead and we should be dead too. We have to find a way to seize some sort of advantage."

"And we need to stay alive," Kevin interrupted.

"We've been running around all day with our backs against the wall. If there's even the slimmest chance we can turn the tables on this situation, we need to try. Don't you see that running and hiding isn't going to get us anywhere out here?" Kate turned around and resumed walking toward the slope.

Standing alone in the woods, Kevin looked up at the cracks between the tree line; the night sky was filled with stars, the breeze was soft, and his only friend left was moving on. Kevin took a deep breath. "This might be my last night on Earth," he murmured to himself. Turning toward Kate, Kevin started to follow.

20:30:04

They slowly crawled on hands and knees toward the edge of the rock face. The mine was in front of them, one hundred feet straight down. The thicket was dense and kept them out of sight. Peering into the clearing, they didn't detect any movement below. Scanning the area, Kevin spotted a small fire near the shed and pointed it out to Kate.

"Where do you think he is?" Kevin whispered.

"I don't know."

Neither moved as they kept their sights fixed on the area near the shed. Everything was silent and still.

"Maybe he's in the shed," Kevin continued.

"Maybe."

Crack!

Kate and Kevin quickly shifted their gazes to the trees left of the fire. A silhouette slowly took form and made its way through the tree line and emerged into the opening. Though they couldn't get a good look at him, it was clear he was younger than the guy they were looking for, and this individual also had a bow and arrow. The man tiptoed timidly toward the fire.

Kevin dropped his head face-first into the grass and then looked up at Kate. "How many more of these people are there?"

"Hello!" the man shouted from below.

Kevin and Kate shifted their gaze back down just in time to see the stocky man who killed Chris emerge from the shed. He made a direct line to the other man and paused a few feet short. They began to talk, but moments later, the conversation escalated, and they began to shout a bit more aggressively, both taking turns gesturing toward the mine entrance.

"Wonder what they're saying," Kevin whispered.

"Oh, I have a hunch," Kate replied.

The men continued to joust at each other, though not ever making any physical contact. Then the new man made a comment, and the other nodded in agreement. *I think he just said, "go right ahead," but I can't be sure.* Kate leaned forward through the thicket.

In a swift move, the newcomer took off his pack, knelt down, removed an object from it, and pointed it straight in the air. Seconds later, a burst of fire rocketed from his hand into the air and exploded above Kate and Kevin's heads.

"A flare?" Kevin asked bewilderedly.

"I didn't see that coming either," Kate whispered.

The flare faded into the night, and again, all was silent. Several minutes passed with neither man saying a word to the other. Then, in a sudden and unexpected turn of events, a third individual emerged from the trees. He was tall and wearing a safari hat.

"Wait, is that Mr. Ranger?" Kevin asked.

"It appears so," Kate muttered. *Well, that solves how we got here.*

Ranger walked up between the two men. All three began to converse; Kevin and Kate could not make out what was being said, but the man who killed Chris was clearly not happy as he spoke; moments later was shouting, and then he stormed off. Emerging from the cabin shortly thereafter, he had his pack on his shoulders, bow in hand, and marched down the hill to the east and disappeared.

Still near the fire, Mr. Ranger made a comment to the other man, who nodded, turned around and started heading back toward where he first emerged from the trees. Ranger didn't move until both men were out of sight, after which he carefully strolled up to the simmering flames near the shed and stamped them out with his boots, but before doing so, he looked up at the rock side and waved.

Kate glared at Kevin. *Did he just wave at us?*

Kevin knew she saw it too. "Screw it, I'm getting some sleep," he muttered as he shifted back from the edge and found a small spot to curl up in the grass.

20:28:58

Mr. Blue made his way through the thicket toward the opening. He had caught the whiff of smoke several minutes prior and opted to investigate. *It's most likely one of the others, but best to confirm.* Bow ready in hand, he cautiously stepped out from the tree cover and into the opening. A small shed stood to the right of the fire as he proceeded forward.

He had spent the day scaling the large hills to the right of their drop zone; he recalled Mr. White headed to the left, and Mr. Black walked off down the middle before he even knew what was happening. The day had been overall uneventful, with the first hill proving somewhat challenging from a terrain perspective, but as he hoped, there were multiple water sources on the descent. The overall experience had been calming and gave him a break from the endless barrage of phone calls, content, and kiss-ass subordinates awaiting him back home. At least it was quiet out here. *Mostly because they took my phone.*

Mr. Blue wondered how Mr. White and Mr. Black had fared during the day. The map they were given detailed a large terrain. From what he could tell, the island was easily over twenty square miles. He hadn't anticipated coming across anyone during the first few hours, but as the day drew on, he began to wonder if the prey were real, and concluded that perhaps the people at APEX intended him to treat them as a metaphor. Nevertheless, Mr. Blue carried on, slowly making his way across the island.

It was close to sunset when he picked up the trail of smoke coming from the hill above. Odds were it was either Mr. Black or Mr. White, but maybe he had struck gold, and the prey were real and unaware of his position. Truth be told, Mr. Blue didn't know what he would do if they were real. The prospect of killing another person wasn't something he yearned to check off his bucket list. The only reason he was on this trip to begin with was because one of his clients back in Texas "got him on a list," whatever that meant.

The calls to begin training had happened as he was told they would, and though he was initially reluctant to play along, he found the preparation invigorating. The thought of separating from his work and duties of the day to focus on survival skills and weapons training challenged a part of his psyche that he had rarely exercised. By the time training was complete, he recalled being quite eager for the hunt to begin, regardless of whether or not what he heard about the excursion was true.

Making his way toward the flame, Mr. Blue decided to make himself known. *Last thing I need is to get shot by one of my own people.* "Hello!" he shouted toward the direction of the flame. Initially, his call was met with silence, but a few seconds later, there was a rumble from the shed to the right of the fire. Mr. Black emerged, quickly making eye contact as he strolled over to Mr. Blue.

"Evening, Mr. Blue," Mr. Black started as he arrived a few feet away. "How's the expedition treating you?

"Oh, so far, uneventful. Looks like you've had a busy day." Mr. Blue gestured toward his watch, indicating he was aware of the score.

"Yea, we had some fireworks over at the farm earlier this afternoon. Overall, short-lived, but definitely the highlight of the day."

"Sorry I missed out." Mr. Blue paused. "Any idea what happened to Mr. White? I see he's no longer competing."

167

Mr. Black shook his head and looked down. "Mr. White made some, uh, tactical errors this afternoon, and he's no longer with us."

"I thought we weren't allowed to tap out unless there were extreme circumstances?"

"Mr. White is dead."

Mr. Blue was shocked to hear the words come from Mr. Black's mouth. He had never truly believed this expedition would put any of the contestants in actual danger. *What else do these people at APEX have planned?*

"It was quick," Mr. Black continued. "I clipped one of them and chased the other two in there." Mr. Black gestured toward the mine shaft entrance.

Mr. Blue squinted and examined the entrance and surrounding landscape. "They're in there now?"

"That's right." Mr. Black glared at Mr. Blue.

"Well, what are we waiting for? Let's go get them." Mr. Blue gestured toward the mine entrance and signaled he was about to approach the door.

"Whoa, whoa, whoa," Mr. Black interjected as he held up his hand. "I can promise you don't want to go in there right now. Also, I have them cornered."

"Meaning what?"

"Meaning you need to go about your business."

"Sounds like my business is in there." Mr. Blue gestured toward the mine.

"Perhaps, but the rules clearly say that a contestant can't interfere with the pursuit of another, and if you take one step further, that's exactly what you'd be doing."

Mr. Blue paused and looked at Mr. Black, who was staring at him with a fierce gaze. *He's not letting me get anywhere near that mine.* Mr. Blue stepped back to ease tension and smiled. Rubbing his chin, he continued, "So let me get this straight: we have the two remaining prey in that tunnel, they're cornered, you're not planning to go in after them, and I'm not allowed to pursue as well?"

"Now, you see, for a moment there I was concerned you weren't nearly as bright as I hoped," Mr. Black replied sarcastically.

"If you're not going to pursue, then I will," Mr. Blue said in a louder voice while pointing to the mine.

"You take another goddamn step toward that mine, and I'll rip your throat out myself, do you hear me?" Mr. Black shouted in response. He took a step forward but restrained himself from taking a second.

Mr. Blue realized the situation was starting to get away from him. He needed to defuse quickly. *Mr. Black is all about the rules, so let's enforce the rules.* Mr. Blue calmly turned back to Mr. Black. "I don't think you and I are going to come to an agreement on the current situation. I think we should escalate."

"Are you serious?" Mr. Black, taken aback, rolled his eyes.

"I formally challenge your claim."

Mr. Black paused, knowing Mr. Blue had just evoked a clear option within the rules. "Suit yourself, go right ahead."

Mr. Blue nodded, bent over, and pulled off his pack. Turning it around, he began to rummage through the main pocket. Seconds later, he removed the flare gun. Mr. Blue examined the gun, then pointed it in the air and fired. The flare shot straight up, leaving a trail of smoke before it made a loud popping explosion several hundred feet above and sizzled as the contents burned off.

Neither man moved for several minutes as they awaited judgment assistance. As anticipated, Ranger emerged shortly thereafter from the hillside. He walked out from the trees and toward the two men, who stood motionless as they stared at their new visitor. "Evening, gentlemen," Ranger said as he arrived between the two. "How may I be of assistance this evening?"

Mr. Blue began to explain that he was under the impression Mr. Black had pursued the two-remaining prey into the mine shaft but was unwilling to proceed further. Mr. Black listened with his arms crossed against his chest. Mr. Blue continued, "In my humble opinion, if Mr. Black isn't willing to pursue, there should be no reason why I can't."

Ranger nodded, making eye contact with Mr. Blue. "Your response, Mr. Black?" he inquired while shifting his attention.

"My response?" Mr. Black chuckled. "My response is your people didn't properly sweep out that mine, and our prey are inside sitting on top of a goddamn box of sweating dynamite."

Mr. Blue abruptly gazed in surprise at Mr. Black. *He never told me about the dynamite.*

"Look, I'm all about keeping this fair," Mr. Black continued. "I gave them until sunrise to come out peacefully, at which point I was planning to set them loose for a bit and then continue the hunt." Mr. Black turned his gaze toward Mr. Blue. "Once they're safely out of the mine, we can continue our pursuits. I'll give them an hour or so to reestablish position, and that'll forgo any possible advantage I'd have up here."

"What if they don't come out by sunrise?"

"Well then, I'll blow them to hell, and our trip is over," Mr. Black snapped. "But I think these kids will come to their senses. They're not stupid."

"Indeed, they're not," Ranger interjected.

"I beg your pardon?" Mr. Black responded.

"If I were to offer an opinion..." Ranger paused. Both men nodded for him to continue. "Your proposal, Mr. Black, is in good faith, but fatally flawed in one key area."

"Which is?"

"You're assuming they're still inside."

Mr. Black went pale, peered back at the mine, and scratched his head. "No way they came through there and I didn't see them."

Mr. Blue smirked and made a concerted effort to conceal his amusement.

"Again, you're assuming that's the only way out," Ranger added.

"Well, isn't it?" Mr. Black replied as he stepped closer to Ranger.

"We honestly don't know. All I can tell you is our systems show they exited the mine some time ago and have since traveled a significant distance."

"Son of a bitch!" Mr. Black yelled as he swatted at plants on the ground with his boot.

"As I see things, there is no formal dispute; neither of you are on a live trail," Ranger concluded. "I think it best that you both pack up and ship out."

Mr. Black was already storming back to the shed. Seconds later, he had his pack and bow in hand, reset his gear, and trudged off down the hill. Mr. Blue and Ranger could make out that he was still cursing to himself as he disappeared into the trees.

"There's something not right about that man," Mr. Blue muttered to Ranger.

"There's something not right with all of you," Ranger replied, "but I hear you about this one." Ranger turned and met Mr. Blue face-to-face. "It's time for you to depart as well. I recommend you head north and keep your distance from Mr. Black for the night."

Mr. Blue nodded, turned around, and walked north into the woods. It wasn't long before Ranger lost sight of Mr. Blue as well.

Ranger walked over to the simmering fire next to the old shed. *Pretty daring of those kids to come back here.* Ranger looked up toward the cliff and gave a casual wave, and then stamped out the fire.

17:09:16

The wind continued to blow softly upon the hilltop. Kevin was sound asleep in the brush and had made little movement for several hours. Kate wanted to sleep, but she couldn't separate her mind from the events of the day. That first night on the mountain where they met Ranger felt like ages ago; truth be told, Kate wasn't entirely sure how many days had elapsed. The only thing certain anymore was that she and Kevin were somehow still alive, and she wasn't sure how to make sense of the day's events. The shock from abruptly waking up in a field with no gear, food or water? Horror from the day's senseless violence? Or, anger toward those who set these events in motion? The weight of all three left her with more than she could process. So instead of sleeping, she sat motionless against a nearby tree and kept watch.

The night had turned silent moments after the three men disappeared into the trees below. She knew of at least three pieces to the puzzle that would need to be solved. The man who killed Chris was likely their biggest problem; he was clearly good at tracking and accurate with a bow. Kate's biggest fear about the stocky man was how amused he had been at the thought of killing. *He headed downhill to the southeast; we need to avoid that direction, assuming he stays course.*

The second man of the evening was a new face to Kate. Tall and slender, he didn't fit the profile of the other two individuals they'd encountered. Kate sensed he wasn't as confident as the others, and that could be a weakness, but it was also what made him dangerous. He was clearly out of his element, and that made him unpredictable. He headed north. *I don't think that's the last we'll see of him before this is all over.*

The final man from below made Kate's blood boil. She had sensed back at camp days before that there was something not quite right about their encounter with Ranger. Though she couldn't nail down precisely what gave her reservations, she remembered observing a similar apprehension in Chris' eyes. Seeing him emerge from the thicket brought a wave of emotions, but also an unnatural sense of relief as Mr. Ranger provided their first connection back to the world that existed outside of this place. Kate was certain he had a heavy hand in their current predicament, but she also wasn't sure to what extent he was an enemy versus ally. She couldn't get over how he directed the two assailants away from where she and Kevin sat. She was equally perplexed by his wave toward them; she was certain that Mr. Ranger knew where they were and chose to send the two men in the opposite directions. *We need to find him—he could be the key to our survival.*

Leaning back against the tree, Kate rocked her head to the left and right, giving her neck a good stretch. The night remained silent, and she wasn't disturbed for some time until she caught the faint sound of movement in the thick below. Alertly dropping into the brush, Kate crawled over to the cliff. Down below, the silhouette of a person walked out of the woods toward the shed. She gazed silently at the tepid motion of the shadow as it made its way across the opening. *The new guy.*

Kate watched as the man approached the shed, peered inside the front door, and cautiously entered. The door creaked as it was pulled shut. Kate waited several minutes for further movement; there was none. *Shelter for the night.* Once she was satisfied that the newcomer wasn't leaving the shed anytime soon, Kate pivoted in the brush and crawled toward Kevin, who was still sound asleep. Grabbing his shoulder, she shook him softly. "Kevin," she whispered.

Kevin quickly awoke, alert and unsure of his surroundings. "What the..." he began to shout as Kate's hand clamped down over his mouth, and she stared into his eyes. Kate whispered to Kevin the news of their visitor.

"I have an idea," Kate whispered, as she gave Kevin a smile.

15:17:16

Mr. Blue awoke to the screaming crash of a burning object breaking through the shed window. Quickly shaken alert, he gazed over at the flaming chunk of wood that broke his sleep. *What the hell?* Springing to his feet, Mr. Blue grabbed his pack, which he was using as a pillow. He made his way toward the bow resting next to the door when a second flaming block crashed through the window on the other side of the shed. Smoke began to fill the cabin as the old structure began to burn.

Reaching for the door, Mr. Blue gave it a strong heave. It didn't budge. Perplexed, he gave the door a second and third heave with greater force. The door didn't move an inch. There was no handle on the inside to work loose; somehow, the door was stuck from the outside. Taking a step back, he kicked the door, which was sturdier than it appeared, and his boot failed to even leave a mark. "Do we have your attention?" a female voice shouted from outside.

"Let me out of here, now!" Mr. Blue shouted as he spun around in the cabin.

"Toss out your weapons first," the voice replied.

"Not happening," Mr. Blue shouted back.

"Then you will burn."

Mr. Blue scrambled through the cottage. The rear was now engulfed in flames; he had a minute at most. Looking around, he tried to find another means of exit. The windows were high and too small for his body. The door was his only way out. The searing heat of the fire waved over Mr. Blue as he raised his hand to shield his face. He began to cough from the smoke. *I have no choice.*

"Okay, let me out!" Mr. Blue shouted as he hacked.

"Weapons first."

Oh, for Christ's sake. Walking up to the left window, he placed the bow between broken shards of glass and shoved it outside. The bow landed with a soft thud on the ground below.

"And your knife."

Reaching to his side, Mr. Blue removed his knife and tossed it out the same window. Seconds later, a creaking sound came from the front door. In a relieved burst, he darted toward the front door, lunged through the opening, and landed face-down in the grass.

A hand reached down and pulled the backpack from his shoulder. Mr. Blue stayed face-down, wheezing and gasping as he attempted to catch his breath. Smoke rose from his hair. The crackling of the wood grew louder as the fire accelerated and engulfed the entire structure. Slowly rolling over onto his back, his face was immediately greeted by the sharp end of an arrow directly in his face. Looking up, the prey, Kate and Kevin, were standing over him.

Neither said a word, both alert to his movement. From the looks of it, they had been through hell. Mr. Blue could clearly make out a serious wound on Kevin's lower calf, and Kate, though intact, had streams of dried blood running from her hairline down her face and past her ear.

"Get up," Kate said as she kept the bow in his face.

Slowly sitting up, Mr. Blue rose to his feet and raised his hands, signaling he surrendered. Not taking his eyes off Kate, Mr. Blue stood motionless.

"Your shoes," she said intently while gesturing the arrowhead toward his feet.

Mr. Blue looked down at his feet. *She can't be serious.*

"Now!" she shouted.

"Okay, okay," Mr. Blue responded as he held up a hand in front of his face, signaling for her to stay calm. Kneeling, Mr. Blue untied his boots. Slowly standing back up, he stepped out of his right boot, then the left, and took a step back. Kevin, who was now sporting Mr. Blue's pack, moved in and grabbed the boots. Mr. Blue didn't move.

"Laces," Kate said to Kevin while nodding at the boots in his hands. Kevin looked down and immediately began to remove the laces. Mr. Blue stood motionless as he watched Kevin untether the boots. The fire was still ablaze behind them.

"Got 'em," Kevin said, holding up the laces for Kate. "What now?"

"His hands," she responded. In a quick motion, she shifted her position to Mr. Blue's right, keeping the arrow intently pointed at his torso.

Kevin cautiously walked up to Mr. Blue and gestured for him to drop his hands and place them out front. Mr. Blue complied. Kevin began to tie his hands together with the boot laces.

"I hope you know what you're doing," Mr. Blue said as Kevin continued to tie his hands.

Kate didn't respond.

"I don't think you do," Mr. Blue continued. "I guarantee they're coming for me right now; they won't let this stand."

"You mean Mr. Ranger," Kevin interrupted, still securing the laces. *How do they know of Ranger?*

"I doubt he's coming," Kate muttered. "Almost finished?" she asked, shifting her gaze toward Kevin.

"All set," Kevin responded as he stepped back from Mr. Blue.

Kate shifted her position back alongside Kevin, never taking her gaze off of Mr. Blue. There was a long pause; nobody spoke. The shed continued to burn as it collapsed in on itself with a loud crash. "Here's how this works," Kate began. "We're going to take a walk. You try to run, you die. You give away our position, you die."

Mr. Blue hesitated, weighing his options. He was outnumbered, hands tied, and had no weapons. But he had APEX on his side, and he wasn't convinced either could hit him on the run with the bow.

In a swift move, Mr. Blue turned and took off. He ran as hard as he could toward the tree line and didn't sense any arrows were fired. *I knew it.*

Almost to the tree line, Mr. Blue accelerated. The sound of quick pounding steps suddenly drew close. Seconds later, something struck his foot mid-stride. He spun and toppled into the first tree along the edge. Crawling up to get leverage, Mr. Blue rolled on his back to stand. Instantly a foot came down on his chest. Kate towered over him. *Collegiate athlete. I forgot that one.*

"Don't do that again," she said as Kevin caught up. Kevin handed her the bow, and she reset the arrow on Mr. Blue. She gestured for Mr. Blue to stand up. "After you."

14:52:35

The sun began to rise over the eastern hills as Kate, Kevin, and Mr. Blue slowly trekked north along the western hillside. Mr. Blue was leading the way, followed closely by Kate, and then Kevin. Kate continued to keep the bow on Mr. Blue's back, occasionally poking him with the tip as a reminder.

Kate was elated their plan had worked. She knew it was a risk to draw the attention of others with the fire, but she believed that it was a reasonable shot to turn the tables in their favor; staying on the hilltop with no tools or means of escape wasn't a long-term solution. The plan was simple, and they had executed it to perfection. The most challenging part of the attack, in her mind, happened after their prisoner surrendered the weapons. Kate was many things, but was she capable of actually shooting another person? It didn't matter, she knew she needed to leave little doubt in the man's mind that she could and would. The entire plan depended on her giving a convincing performance.

"Neither of you are getting off this island alive," Mr. Blue said as he broke the silence, still marching forward.

"What makes you say that?" Kate responded.

Pausing, Mr. Blue turned and faced Kate and Kevin. "What do you think is going on here?"

Neither said a word.

"This is all a game. None of this is real," Mr. Blue continued. "You two. You're the game."

Kevin recalled the red sheet from APEX. "What is APEX?"

"They're the ones who put this on." Mr. Blue smiled. "You were selected as our targets. We were put on this island to track you." Mr. Blue paused and scratched his chin with his bound hands. "Truth be told, I wasn't sure until recently if you even existed, and if you did, I thought you might be actors playing out some sort of elaborate interactive role-play. But I can see that's clearly not the case, and they actually expected us to track and take you down."

"Who are the 'we' and 'us' in that statement?" Kate interrupted.

"Mr. White, Mr. Black, and I," he continued, "and from the sounds of it, you two are already well acquainted with Mr. Black."

"And there's nobody else?" Kate continued.

"Not that I know of, but who knows, working with these people," Mr. Blue concluded.

"What kind of person would even consider a game like this?" Kevin replied.

"They offered multiple scenarios upfront. In my line of business, when contacts give you access to something like this, you do it. I picked this excursion because it best fit my schedule."

Kate and Kevin paused and looked at each other briefly. "How does the game work?" Kate asked.

Mr. Blue explained the scoring system, what the timers on their watches signified, and how he needed to reach the extraction before time expired. Mr. Blue motioned down to his blue watch as he explained the countdown. Kevin and Kate were taken aback by his candor as he continued to explain the stakes and the buy-ins. "That's why again I say, neither of you are getting off this island alive."

"But there is a way out of here, you just mentioned the extraction," Kevin replied.

"That's assuming you can get across this island without crossing paths with Mr. Black, and also assumes they'll let you get on that helicopter."

"The rules we were given said we won if we survived," Kevin added.

"Again, a big if," Mr. Blue responded.

"So far your mistake has been underestimating us," Kate interrupted. "When this game, as you call it, started, we were three on three. It would now appear we have an advantage." She met his eyes until the smile left his face. "Now, let's start with getting the location right. I bet you know how to get us to extraction, don't you?"

Mr. Blue didn't respond, though Kate caught him gazing down in the direction of his cargo pants pocket. Kate quickly moved forward and drove her hand into his pocket. Mr. Blue didn't move. Seconds later, she removed her hand, grasping a piece of paper.

Returning her attention to Mr. Blue, she handed the paper over to Kevin, who quickly opened it up. "It's a map," he said. "Sure looks like this island. There's the farm, the hills. Yeah, it's all here."

"Show us the extraction point," Kate said to Mr. Blue as she gestured Kevin forward.

With both hands still tied, Mr. Blue pointed to a spot at the top of the island. "There's no chance you two will make it," he said, looking up at Kate.

"What are these?" Kevin asked while gesturing to small black lines going through the map at various spots on the island. Each was marked with a capital letter.

"Those are emergency exit points, in case of weather and such," Mr. Blue replied. "I'm pretty sure that's how Ranger and his team get around as well."

Kate leaned forward and looked at the map. "Where are we right now?"

"Right here," Kevin said, pointing down at the hills on the left side of the map.

"And there's an exit right there, Exit E, to the northeast," Kate added.

"Looks like it."

"Then let's start there," Kate concluded. Kevin nodded in agreement. They both peered down at the map and continued to evaluate their path and potential obstacles they'd face en-route.

As they continued to examine the map, Mr. Blue, taking advantage of their diverted attention, began to slowly inch backward. The laces around his hand were finally ready after he'd carefully tugged at them for the previous few minutes. Kate had lowered her guard, and it was now or never.

Mr. Blue lunged forward and drove his shoulder into Kevin and sent him rolling down the hill. Quickly pivoting, he dove at Kate, knocking her off her feet. He quickly gained leverage on her, broke his hands free, rolled her onto her back, and began to raise his hands to strike. Kate shifted to block as he came down. Absorbing a lot of the blow with her arms, she reached down and sank her teeth into Mr. Blue's arm. He cried out as he pulled back on his assault. Quickly moving, Kate rolled onto her stomach and began to crawl and survey the ground.

Wasting little time, Mr. Blue reestablished his position and scurried after Kate. "No, you don't," he said as he grabbed her ankle and slowed her crawl. She kicked at him with her boots as she continued to survey the ground. Mr. Blue dodged her strikes and climbed up on her again. With both hands, he grabbed her sides and began to flip her on her back again. Kate struggled, but Mr. Blue had leverage and continued to roll her over. Seconds later she was again on her back, and Mr. Blue brought his hands down on her neck. Kate frantically waved her hand across the surrounding ground. *Please be something, please be there... Got you.*

Clutching a stone, Kate raised her fist and swiftly struck Mr. Blue across the right temple. He immediately fell off of Kate, who scrambled to her feet. On his hands and knees, Mr. Blue struggled to open his eyes, slightly shaking his head back and forth. Blood ran down along his hairline where the rock made contact. Kate, breathing heavily, walked around Mr. Blue and called for Kevin, who was already scrambling to his feet and scaling back up the hill. Kate turned back to Mr. Blue and, in a surging lunge, drove her boot into his crouching stomach. Mr. Blue collapsed to his side in a fetal position.

Kevin quickly joined Kate. "You good?"

"Yeah," she replied, staring down at Mr. Blue, who began to roll back on his knees, spitting blood into the dirt.

"That's it," he muttered, "I'm done."

Kate and Kevin kept their attention on Mr. Blue, assuming he would try something again.

"You hear me?!" Mr. Blue shouted in the air. "I'm done, I forfeit, get me out of here!"

"Who are you talking to?" Kevin asked.

Mr. Blue didn't answer as he looked up at Kevin and Kate and then leaned back in the dirt.

***

Holding their position for a half-hour, Kevin and Kate opted to use Mr. Blue's capitulation to rest. The sun was beginning to shine over the hill, and the temperature rose with it. Kate was actually curious if someone would come to Mr. Blue's aid after he shouted. To her delight and suspicion, nobody came.

Kate stood and looked over at Kevin, who sat hunched against a nearby tree. "Alright, let's move on."

Kevin nodded and began to stand.

"I'm not going anywhere," Mr. Blue muttered.

"Sorry to burst your bubble, but you're absolutely coming with us," Kate replied.

Mr. Blue sat up and looked directly at Kate; dried blood covered his face, and dirt and twigs were tangled in his hair.

"Face it, they're not coming," she continued. "You're alone out here."

Mr. Blue smirked. "None of us are alone out here." Turning, Mr. Blue put his arm on a nearby tree and slowly stood, struggling to find his balance. He started to laugh as he walked closer to Kate and Kevin. "Take a closer look," he said, pointing to the neck of his shirt.

Glaring closely, Kevin made out exactly what Mr. Blue was pointing toward.

Smiling, Mr. Blue gestured to Kevin. "He gets it." Kate continued to stare at the shirt. "We're on camera," Mr. Blue continued, "you, me, the others, we've been recorded since we set foot on this island. Every move, every step has been captured, logged, and analyzed."

Kate wasn't surprised to hear they were being tracked, not after the story Mr. Blue had shared regarding the expedition. "This changes nothing," she said. "We're moving."

"I don't think so," Mr. Blue replied.

Kate smiled and walked up to meet Mr. Blue face-to-face. "Do I need to break your nose as well to get my point across?"

Mr. Blue smiled and stepped back, bracing himself on the tree behind him. "Do your worst."

Kate didn't move. *He's calling my bluff.*

"That's what I thought," Mr. Blue replied as he shook his head and chuckled.

Kate turned around and began to walk away. Mr. Blue didn't move and continued to enjoy the moment.

No rules. Pivoting quickly, Kate took aim with her bow, and released the arrow at Mr. Blue, who immediately let out a scream. The arrow struck directly through his forearm and into the tree. Mr. Blue continued to scream.

"What the hell, Kate?" Kevin said as he joined her side.

She didn't respond or acknowledge his comment. She stared at the screaming man wiggling against the tree. *What did I just do?*

"You bitch!" Mr. Blue screamed as he flailed his free arm into the air. Tears began to run down his face.

Kate slowly approached Mr. Blue and met him again, face-to-face. This time Mr. Blue didn't break eye contact and kept a straight face. "Let's try this again," Kate began. "You're coming with us, or the next one lands right here." Kate flicked his forehead between the eyes.

Mr. Blue stared at her in terror, still heavily panting from the shock he was experiencing. He looked over at Kevin, who was also staring intently at Kate. Looking back at Kate, Mr. Blue nodded.

"See," she said as she grabbed his arm and, with a quick jerk, removed the arrow from the tree, "that wasn't so hard." She grabbed Mr. Blue by the shoulder and gestured for him to start walking. With no shoes, an arrow in his arm, and the throbbing headache that was undoubtedly the result of a concussion, Mr. Blue led Kevin and Kate north toward Exit E.

13:41:04

"We have to do something," one of the techs shouted over to the Broker. Staring up at the main screen, the Broker agreed. *Has this gone too far?* He looked over at the analyst. "My hands are tied; we need to consult the panel." Leaning forward, the Broker reached for his red phone, set the receiver to his ear with his left hand, and pressed #1.

He leaned back in his chair. "Yes, I'm looking at the screen right now. Uh-huh." The Broker paused and listened to the other end of the phone. "Do we have grounds? Uh-huh, that's what I was thinking as well." Leaning forward, the Broker prepared to end the call. "Yes, agreed, I'll tell him." The Broker hung up the red phone and looked over to the nearby analysts. "Find me Ranger."

"One second, sir," the analyst to his right responded. The screen quickly shuffled between island locations, shifting from tunnels and landscape to a live stream overlooking Ranger, who was now on the main screen standing in a field.

"Go," Ranger said, as he tapped his ear.

"It's me," the Broker began. "So two things. First, I got your report on Mr. Black."

"And..."

"Background check didn't find anything terribly unusual. Wealthy family, private schools most of his childhood. There was one incident

186

involving the killing of local pets, but aside from a single infraction, his record is clear. Spent his entire adult life traveling and acquiring startup businesses. He frequently goes by several other aliases, some of which have been linked to various crimes, though none substantiated."

"Let me guess, assault..."

"And murder," the Broker continued, "but again, this didn't officially trigger an audit on our end because he was never formally charged or linked to the crimes. You know how it is with these people and the types of contacts they make for exclusive access to contraband and such. Rich people also always deal with a slew of litigation in their lives as others swipe in for quick extortion settlements. Happens all the time."

"I hate to burst your bubble," Ranger interrupted, "but he has all the markings of a sadist."

"No, I wouldn't go that far," the Broker quickly responded.

"I'm going to disagree, especially if we have actual charges regarding animal cruelty, followed by a pattern of escalating accusations into adulthood. This is not a guy we want to associate our brand with, and we certainly don't need him running around this park with lethal weapons. I've already caught him toying with two of the prey, and recent footage showed he threatened Mr. Blue. He's a predator, Broker."

"Well, then you're going to love this next part," the Broker replied. "The judges are invoking The Diversion Protocol."

"Jesus Christ, where?"

"Exit E."

"Right, I'm on my way, over and out." Ranger tapped his ear and walked out of sight on the screen.

"Send the message," the Broker said as he leaned back in his chair. *Now things get interesting.*

***

Mr. Black trudged through the open field, looking for any sign of movement. After the events of the previous night, he opted to head south and check the perimeter of the island. All was quiet. It was there he set up camp and decided to get some sleep before the home stretch push. He was still frustrated that Kate and Kevin had gotten the better of him in the mine. *A mistake that won't happen a second time.*

Buzz. Buzz.

Mr. Black looked down at his watch to read the update. Mr. Blue better not have tagged them.

Diversion Protocol – Exit E

Mr. Black looked up at the sky. The weather couldn't be more perfect. *Why are they asking me to make my way to the other side of the island? Exit C is much closer.* Mr. Black looked down at his watch again and quickly surmised the context of the message.

"Outstanding," he said to himself as he smiled and turned his vector north.

11:13:55

I took them several hours to reach the edge of the central field. Opting to stay out of the direct sunlight, Kate directed Mr. Blue and Kevin to stay up on the hill as they trekked forward. The treetops blocked the sun's rays as they had the day before, and Kate surmised the hillside provided an advantage should Mr. Black decide to attack from below. They made a few pit stops along the way. It was Kevin who discovered Mr. Blue's rations of food in the pack; they had never been more excited to dive into a bag of freeze-dried pasta, though they had to eat it cold because Kate insisted that on this island smoke frequently drew a crowd. With the field in sight, they carefully descended the hill and paused at the tree line.

Kate knelt and surveyed the field. Lightly covered for several hundred meters of mostly flat terrain, the area appeared to succumb to thicker growth on the eastern side. "Let me see the map," she said to Kevin.

Peering down, the map confirmed her suspicions. "We're north of the farm; that's the field of hay we saw yesterday when we approached the farm from the river." She pointed to the farm on the map as Kevin nodded.

"Exit E should be somewhere right in front of us, right?"

"Somewhere in there," she replied as she pointed toward the overgrown field.

Mr. Blue sat silently in the brush.

Standing up, Kate folded the map and put it in her pocket. "Let's go," she said while gesturing Kevin and Mr. Blue to stand.

Cautiously entering the field, they slowly made their way toward the overgrown farming plot. Kevin struggled with the heat, and his leg was now throbbing after miles of hiking; he did his best not to give away his discomfort to Kate or Mr. Blue. The trek across the field toward the overgrowth only took a few minutes; neither Kate nor Kevin could recall the last time they had marched on flat terrain. They would have arrived at the overgrown field even faster had it not been for Mr. Blue staggering and dragging his feet as he crossed.

Arriving at the edge of the old farming plot, Kevin and Kate quickly looked along the edge for anything foreign or out of place that could signal an exit. Nothing appeared in sight. Straight ahead was a dense field of overgrown vegetation; among them were stalks of corn. The field's growth was tall and thick, up to Kevin's chest in most places.

Kevin looked into the field and shook his head. "I think we should split up," he said to Kate.

"You must be joking," she replied.

"The entrance isn't out here, which means it's somewhere in there. We'll cover more ground and increase our chances if we split up."

Kate looked apprehensively at Kevin and then peered into the thick.

"I don't like it either," Kevin continued, "but you said it yourself, the only way we're getting out of here alive is if we take calculated risks."

Kate knew Kevin was right. Despite his lack of outdoor skills, he was a pragmatic problem-solver, and it didn't help that he used her own philosophy to sell the proposal. "How do you want to do this?"

"I'm thinking we go straight in, moving slowly, keeping close enough to each other that we don't need to yell to communicate. You can go in right here; I'll head twenty paces up and do the same."

"And what of our friend?" Kate gestured toward Mr. Blue.

"You've now kicked his ass twice," Kevin replied while smiling at Mr.

Blue. "He's all yours. My advice would be to remove him from the game if he gives you any problems."

Kate smiled at Kevin as he turned and marched along the field line. It didn't take him long to find a suitable position just north of Kate and Mr. Blue. Turning around, he waved to Kate.

"All set," Kate replied with a nod and motioned for Mr. Blue to enter the brush. Slowly, all three entered the farming plot. Kate kept her head on a swivel, examining the ground with each step while keeping tabs on Mr. Blue. *If he tries anything...*

The sun beat down on them as they slowly trudged through the thicket. Small flies and insects jumped and flew around their heads with each step. "Anything yet?" Kate tried not to shout. They had been in the field for no more than a few minutes, and she knew he would have alerted her had he found anything, but ascertaining his position brought her comfort.

"Nothing yet," Kevin replied.

Kate continued to carefully survey the field. *If the map was correct, it's right in this area; if we keep walking, we're going to pass it altogether.*

"Hey Kate!" Kevin said a little too loudly.

"What's up?"

There was a long pause—Kevin didn't answer.

"Kevin, what's up?" She turned toward his direction; he was nowhere in sight. She paused and waited for a response.

For the second time, Kevin did not answer. With her pulse now pounding, Kate aggressively nudged Mr. Blue north toward the general location of Kevin. *I don't like this.* She pushed Mr. Blue in the back with her arrowhead and told him to pick up the pace. Moments later, they were in the general location she thought Kevin would be. She spun frantically, searching for any sign of Kevin.

"Kevin, where are you?" she shouted.

"I'm over here," Kevin finally responded.

"Where?" Kate asked while swiveling her head.

"Here," Kevin said as he jumped up and down.

Peering around, Kate spotted Kevin jumping up and down several paces ahead. Quickly adjusting, she pushed Mr. Blue toward Kevin. As they approached his position, the field opened up into a dirt and stone-covered patch. At its center was an angled box with a door. It was a storm cellar. Kevin stood in front of the door and waved Kate over. The cellar had two brown doors that started at ground level and angled up across the terrain. The other end of the entrance was roughly knee-high. Arriving at Kevin's side, she examined what he found.

"Funny, isn't it," Kevin said.

"What?"

"Look at the lock," he replied.

Peering closer, Kate immediately let out a deep sigh. The doors themselves were clearly very old, but in the center sat a shiny open padlock.

"Looks like the same one from the mine, no?" Kevin added.

"It's the same," Kate muttered.

"Should we open her up?" Kevin continued.

Kate didn't reply as she stepped forward onto the storm cellar and took a closer look. She quickly swiveled and looked at Mr. Blue. "You," she said, "get over here."

Mr. Blue reluctantly complied and slowly walked over to where Kate stood.

"Open it."

Crouching down, Mr. Blue grabbed the left cellar door with his good arm and heaved the door open. It flew back with a crack. Mr. Blue peered inside. "Nuh-uh," Kate said to Mr. Blue as she grabbed his shoulder and pulled him back. "Get your ass over there." Turning around, she pushed him to the ground next to the storm cellar.

Kevin walked to the opening and peered inside. There was a staircase, no more than ten steps, and then a passageway that quickly faded into black several feet later. "Where does it go?" Kevin asked Mr. Blue.

"No clue," Mr. Blue replied. "I was told the door was here in the event of an emergency, that's all."

Kate walked around to the back of the storm cellar and began to ponder their next move. *Obviously, we need to go in. But who knows what's down there, and the tight space reduces our chances of any plausible escape.* She looked up to the sky and took a deep breath; this decision would likely determine their fate. She peered off to the south. In the distance, she could make out the top of the farm and barn from the previous day. She shook her head; so much had transpired since their time in the farmhouse. Shifting her gaze to the left, she caught a glimpse of a flicker close by. Pausing, she looked at the spot again. Again, there was a flicker. *Looks like the sun is refracting off of something— Wait, I've seen this before.*

"Kevin, get down!" she screamed as she dropped to her knees and rolled behind the storm cellar. Crawling around the corner, she saw Kevin dodge and fall to the ground as an arrow whisked passed him and stuck into the right door of the cellar.

"Shit, there he goes," Kevin yelled, pointing at the storm cellar. Kate quickly looked over and caught the top of Mr. Blue's head descending into the tunnel.

"Go after him!" she shouted at Kevin as she crawled toward the front of the cellar door. Kevin paused. "I'm right behind you," Kate added.

Kevin quickly pivoted to his knees and hopped down into the cellar.

Despite the adrenaline rush from the events at hand, Kate knew exactly what she had to do. *If I follow him, whoever is shooting at us will continue to pursue us.* Kate looked over at the right door, still closed, with the open padlock on top. Going to her knees, Kate darted to the open door. Kevin stood at the bottom of the steps looking up.

"Let's go!" he shouted.

"We need to lock this door!"

"He's getting away," Kevin pointed down the tunnel.

"Kevin, he's here. If I don't lock this door, we all die," she replied. "Get after him!" Kate reached for her pocket and tossed him the knife she acquired from Mr. Blue.

Kevin paused, but Kate could tell he knew she was right. "Fine, but take this," he replied while throwing up the pack with their remaining arrows. "I'll see you soon."

"Go! Head north, I'll meet you at the extraction point," she shouted as she closed the cellar door, slid across the top, and clicked the padlock into place. Seeing the door was secure, she rolled off of the door and ran into the field with a bag and bow in hand.

10:50:02

Keeping her head below the brush line, Kate swiftly made her way across the field toward the western trees. The cellar door was safely locked, but she knew Mr. Black was close by, and she no longer had any cover that could slow an arrow. She didn't have time to worry about the noise she was making; she knew the brush moving around her surely made it easy for Mr. Black to follow. Without looking back, she continued to push forward, keeping her head as low as possible.

"Hey, sweetheart!" Mr. Black suddenly shouted. "I can see you moving over there!"

Kate immediately paused. *This isn't going to work; every move I make gives away my position.* Pausing, Kate stopped her advance and began to evaluate her options. Nearby plants continued to sway as a light breeze swept across the field. Looking up, Kate saw there was a cluster of clouds rolling in. She sighed in relief. *At least I'm now out of the sun.*

"Clever move, locking your friend down there," Mr. Black shouted again. "I'll get to him shortly."

She needed to think of something. *If I can get him to shoot, that might give me a chance to return fire.* Looking around for anything that could attract his attention, she immediately remembered that Kevin had handed her Mr. Blue's pack. Swiveling around, she quickly took it off and set it to her side. Taking a deep breath, she pulled an arrow from the back and set it on the bow. *Okay, 3... 2... 1.*

Using her left hand, she lifted the pack above the grass line. Almost instantly, an arrow struck it with surprising force and drove the pack from Kate's hand. *Now I know approximately where he is.* Quickly standing, she caught a clear view of Mr. Black reloading. Clutching the bow, she drew, fired, and then dropped back to the ground.

"Whoa ho ho!" Mr. Black shouted as he began to laugh. "You're going to have to do better than that, sweetheart; what else you got?"

Shit.

It was time to move. Mr. Black wasn't going to give her a second opportunity using the bag as a diversion. Quickly crawling forward, she did her best to minimize disturbing the surrounding growth, though she was sure Mr. Black continued to follow her moves. Up ahead, she spotted a break in the growth and lunged forward.

Her knees were scraped from landing on a patch of coarse dirt and gravel. Peering to her left and right, she quickly realized where she was. *A trail.* Slightly overtaken by the nearby growth from both sides, the trail ran north and south through the field; clearly used by the farmers back when the field was actively worked. Pausing, she evaluated her next move. *What are the odds Mr. Black knows of this trail?* Leaning down toward the pack, Kate removed three arrows and then set the pack upright against the brush on the far side of the trail. Grabbing the arrows, she silently ducked south along the trail, making as little sound as possible.

As she quietly scurried south along the trail, Mr. Black slowly approached the general area where she'd left the pack. *He still thinks I'm up there. If I keep moving, I can reach a safe distance and head to the trees.* Kate peered over her shoulder to the tree line approximately a quarter mile away. *But what about Kevin?* Kate knew if she gave Mr. Black the slip for a second time, he would go after Kevin, and who knew how he was faring down in those tunnels as it was. *I know what I have to do.*

Pausing, Kate turned, went to one knee, and loaded the bow. She had a clear line on the pack, some fifty feet up the trail. *No more running.* She looked up at the sky and took a deep breath, presuming it could likely be her last such moment.

Mr. Black quietly approached the pack with a smile on his face. Breaking through the brush to the trail, he quickly realized the pack was unaccompanied. Alertly swiveling left, Mr. Black began to look for any sign of Kate, then turned to his right. It was at that moment he and Kate met eye-to-eye once again. Taking a deep breath, Kate drew and released the arrow at her target.

Mr. Black screamed in pain as the arrow struck his face. He immediately toppled down to the ground, cursing and screaming. Not interested in pressing her luck, Kate stood and ran away toward the tree line, her bow and two remaining arrows in hand. As she looked back across the field, there was no sign of Mr. Black. She picked up her pace and, moments later, disappeared into the trees and began to scale the hill. For the first time since landing on the island, Kate was alone.

10:38:21

Hobbling through the dark passageway, Kevin had completely lost sight of Mr. Blue. To Kevin's surprise, the tunnel was equipped with modern lighting that ran along the top left corner of the tunnel wall, flickering every few moments. The tunnel itself had also transformed from a musty subterranean storage-like space, to a modern, paved network, closely resembling an underground sewer system without the water. Kevin knew he didn't have time to worry about what this all meant; he had concluded this was likely part of the APEX installation to assist with crew movements and such, and that would suffice for now.

The passage initially ran north and south, as far as Kevin could tell, but had since branched off at a few junctures. Kevin had previously stopped at once such point to see if there were any signs of Mr. Blue; to his disappointment, there was no evidence anyone had been nearby in quite some time, which gave Kevin pause to continue. It was the thought of Kate locking herself out in the field with Mr. Black that kept him going; she had entrusted him with the task of reacquiring Mr. Blue, and he knew he couldn't fail.

Keeping alert to his surroundings, Kevin continued limping down the tunnel, the army knife set in hand. The lights continued to flicker as a faint breeze hollowed down the tunnel. "And, this is the part where a monster jumps out, and I die an unfortunate yet predictable death," Kevin whispered under his breath. Continuing forward, Kevin approached another break in the tunnel.

To his left, the tunnel turned dark. *Not going down there.* To his right, the tunnel opened up to a large room with beams running onto the floor. "Is that sunlight?" he said to himself as a loud clunk echoed from inside. Taking a big gulp, Kevin turned to his right and slowly entered the room.

Looking around, Kevin quickly observed he was no longer standing in a modern structure; from the looks of it, the room was the basement of an old building. Sunlight crept through multiple vents across the ceiling. The smell of must immediately struck his nose as he entered the room.

"Watch out for the pipes on the floor," a voice spoke as Kevin entered. Peering across the room, Kevin immediately made out the source: Mr. Blue was sitting against the far wall, panting, holding a bloody shin, his arm still sporting an arrow. To his left a was a small pipe that came up from the floor and ran through the left side of the room; Mr. Blue had clearly not seen it and taken a severe fall. Kevin, looking over his shoulders, cautiously walked toward Mr. Blue.

"Looks like you've caught me again," Mr. Blue sighed as he rolled his head back against the wall, sweat running down his face.

"What is this place?" Kevin asked.

"A room, Mr. Wu," Mr. Blue replied.

The room was unremarkable: cement walls on all sides, and the vents above were the only lead to the outside world. Looking up from Mr. Blue, Kevin caught a square object nestled on the far wall. He moved closer. Mr. Blue didn't flinch; he was clearly struggling to keep his eyes open, and the trauma on his body left him virtually incapacitated. Moving closer, Kevin quickly saw the object on the far wall was a steel naming plate. Inches away, he began to make out the faded words that were once vibrantly pressed into its side.

Author A.G.R. Mining Company
Pittsburgh, Pennsylvania, United States of America
Established 1854

Stepping back from the wall, Kevin knew this could be the key to everything. "This is it," he said.

"What do you mean?" Mr. Blue asked as he rolled his head against the wall and peered up at Kevin.

"This is who settled the island. They built the mines, maybe even the farmhouse. This means when we get off this island..."

"If, if you get off this island," Mr. Blue interrupted.

"When we get off, we can find this place again. This terrain is unique for an island already, now we have a previous owner and possibly the original settler."

Mr. Blue sighed and rolled his head back and forth on the wall. "There were hundreds of mining companies in that era, and thousands of mining locations all over the world. It's not enough."

"No, it is," a voice interrupted from the entrance of the room. Quickly turning around, Kevin easily made out the silhouette of Mr. Ranger walking into the room.

"About damn time you boys showed up," Mr. Blue muttered. "See what these little shits did to me," he continued while holding up his arm, an arrow sticking straight through it.

"This was originally an experimental limestone mining station," Ranger continued. "Didn't last long, though, after a few accidents and the discovery of an underground river." Ranger walked forward.

"And you acquired the land from them?" Kevin asked.

"The land has changed hands many times over the past century." Ranger continued forward, gesturing Kevin to the side as he began to examine and dust the plate with his hand. "Who owns what is inconsequential to people like us." Ranger looked over to Kevin, and then down at the knife in his hands. "Can you put that away?"

Kevin didn't reply and looked down at Mr. Blue, who was eagerly staring at Ranger. "So, what happens now?"

"What happens now is we leave," Ranger replied as he walked around Kevin and offered his hand to Mr. Blue, who hadn't moved from his place along the wall. Mr. Blue extended his hand in return, and Ranger helped him to his feet. Kevin watched as Mr. Blue ascended against the wall, grimacing the entire time. Ranger grabbed Mr. Blue's good arm and flung it around his shoulder. "Follow me."

Exiting the room, Ranger and Mr. Blue turned right back into the modern hall and began to slowly limp forward. Kevin followed.

"You build all of this?" Kevin said, breaking the silence.

"Four hundred tons of concrete poured, and three shift rotations over a four-month development schedule went into preparing this island," Ranger replied without turning around.

"Is this how you get around?"

"One of the ways," Ranger added.

"Where are we headed?"

"To the extraction point," said Ranger as he paused and turned back to Kevin. "But there's something you should see first." Ranger pointed to a door to his left.

"What's in there?" Elated that Ranger was taking him to the extraction point, Kevin approached the door.

"Let me show you," Ranger said as he gently set Mr. Blue down against the opposite tunnel wall. Turning back to the door, he gave the door's circular metal crank a turn and heaved it open. Ranger entered first, and Kevin followed close behind.

"The farm and mine are the island's only standing structures that remain, but it's clear to us that this was once a vibrant mining station. We found all sorts of these underground storage rooms during excavation," Ranger began as he walked into the dark room. Looking around,

Kevin made out four walls, no windows or sources of light. The ground was made of gravel, and the familiar whiff of must filled the air. "Some of these locations were packed to the ceiling with excavation tools and equipment," Ranger continued. "Others, like this one, clearly had one purpose."

Kevin walked forward into the room. "And what's that?"

Ranger turned and pointed to the ceiling. Looking up, Kevin quickly made out what appeared to be a series of bars behind a slab of cement.

"We sealed it during construction," Ranger said as he turned and looked at Kevin and sighed. "I genuinely wish you hadn't seen that plaque in the other room." Ranger began to circle Kevin, his back now against the door, and Kevin's against the far wall of the room. "You put up one hell of a fight out there. Most of us had you pegged as the first to go, but you just kept on battling, even through your injury." Ranger paused and pointed down at Kevin's leg. "You earned the right to leave this place, of that I'm sure."

"So, what's the problem?"

"The problem is you saw something you weren't supposed to see in that other room. You now know this place, who built it, and a man with your intellect will pinpoint this location from any laptop or smartphone in a matter of minutes." Ranger stepped forward and placed his hand on Kevin's shoulder. "Forgive me." Ranger smiled at Kevin and then swatted the knife from his hand and drove his fist into his stomach, knocking Kevin to the ground. Ranger turned and made his way to the exit.

Rolling around, Kevin lifted his head to see Ranger closing the door behind him.

"I'm sorry," Ranger said as the door slammed shut and the lock clicked. The room was now pitch black and silent. Kevin was alone and going nowhere.

***

On the other side of the door, Ranger stood motionless and upset with the turn of events. Lightly pounding his fist on the door, he turned and offered a hand to Mr. Blue. Helping Mr. Blue to his feet, Ranger gestured for them to continue moving north up the tunnel.

"Where are we headed?" Mr. Blue asked.

"Extraction." Ranger looked over at the limping Mr. Blue. "Nothing's changed."

"What happens to him?" Mr. Blue said as he gestured to the locked door.

"We'll take it from here," Ranger muttered.

Mr. Blue paused and smiled. "Any chance I can convince you to tell the judges I locked him in there on my own?"

Ranger paused and looked at Mr. Blue. After everything he'd been through, Mr. Blue had learned nothing; he was still the man he was going into the excursion and only had victory on his mind. Ranger shook his head. "If my memory serves me, you openly quit several hours ago," Ranger began. "I distinctly remember watching you jumping up and down, yelling you quit and wanted out."

"So you were there," Mr. Blue responded, "and you let them do all of this to me."

"What happened to you," Ranger said, "you brought on all by yourself."

Mr. Blue went silent as Ranger brushed his good arm free.

"I think you can handle the rest of this by yourself," Ranger continued. "Straight ahead, you'll come to a stairwell; our team will be waiting for you there." Ranger pointed straight ahead.

Mr. Blue stood motionless as he looked at Ranger, who turned and walked the other way. Mr. Blue watched him for some time until Ranger turned a corner and disappeared. Looking forward, Mr. Blue used the wall as a crutch and pushed forward.

***

Ranger rounded the corner and tapped his ear. "I need a removal team in Block F2." He paused. "And tell them to make it quick... yes, a black bag." Ranger shook his head and continued to walk with a hand near his ear, "I don't care how you do it. Mr. Blue is also in the north tunnel, making his way to extraction; make sure an escort meets him. He also needs medical attention." Ranger paused in frustration as he continued to listen through his earpiece. "Of course he's disqualified; we have him openly quitting on camera, he has an arrow through his forearm, and he can't even walk." Ranger nodded, and then began to walk again. "Got it. Over and out."

10:01:02

Mr. Black stared up at the cloudy sky as a breeze slowly caressed his face. The previous series of events had not unfolded as he expected. He was alive, but unable to get the taste of fiberglass out of his mouth. Sitting up, Mr. Black had an arrow running through his left cheek. Thinking back to the events that had unfolded, he agreed Kate made a bold move using the trail to mask her location. The shot was spot on. It was by the grace of God, or pure dumb luck, that he somehow avoided the brunt of her attack.

Sitting up, Mr. Black looked down at the arrow hanging from his mouth. The shaft was running along his tongue, with the arrowhead protruding several inches outside his left cheek. *That's about as close as you get.* Crouching over and gritting his teeth, he grabbed the arrow and carefully pulled. Seconds later, the arrow was free, and his cheek and inner mouth began to bleed. He sighed from the pain and took a moment to breathe. Looking down at the ground, he spit a mouthful of blood.

Buzz. Buzz.

Mr. Black looked down at his wristwatch.

Mr. Black - 500 Points

Mr. White - 200 Points

Mr. Blue - 0 Points

Please proceed to extraction.

Mr. Black smirked and looked up at the sky. Gazing back down at his watch, he counted as the seconds as they disappeared. *9:58:31. 9:59:30. 9:58:29...*

"Like hell I will," he said to himself as he gathered his pack, wiped the fresh blood from his cheek, and started slowly marching toward the western tree line.

8:51:12

Kate looked down at her watch and then back to the open map she had in her left hand. If she was reading it correctly, the hill would slope down ahead and bottom out into light forest. From there, if she headed north, she would hit water in about two miles. The extraction point was on the north end of the island, and she could follow the water around to the drop, which appeared to be an open field near a dock.

Alternatively, she could head west to Exit A and possibly catch up with Kevin. She wondered how Kevin was faring and weighed the risk of doubling back to assist him versus making her way to extraction. The distances were essentially the same, both requiring a downhill trek and a few miles of flat, forested terrain.

Kate continued to weigh her options. Had Kevin caught up with Mr. Blue? Did he need her help? The primary risk of heading west was missing him altogether. There was also the time component; even if they made it to extraction, they still needed to survive until all of the time expired. *Eight hours is an eternity out here.* Kate paused, contemplating her options once more. *I did tell him to meet me at extraction to the north. So, that's what he's likely doing.* Folding up the map, Kate made her decision. *North it is.*

The day had drawn long, and the overcast sky had grown darker, leaving relatively little sunlight on the forest floor. Timing wasn't critical, from an extraction standpoint; she still had over eight hours, and by her estimate the dock was at most a three-hour hike, especially if the terrain was mostly downhill or flat. The shadow that covered the forest floor had brought a sense of calm to Kate, as did the elation of finally escaping perpetual pursuit. Her adrenaline had started to wear off, her eyes heavy and her body aching.

Kate looked down at her watch once more and quickly realized she had been awake for over twenty-four hours. The events of the past day were still beyond her comprehension. Chris was gone. The episode in the cave could have easily ended violently. And most recently, the field. *Did I kill a person?* Part of her regretted not running over to check; if nothing else, she could have reclaimed her pack. Her stomach growled. *I should have definitely retrieved the pack before leaving; there was still a pouch of food inside.* Instinctively, she knew going back would have forced her to confront the result of her actions. She knew the arrow had struck Mr. Black; she remembered his screams as he dropped. Had she run to the trees for safety, or was she running from herself?

Deciding to take a quick break, Kate found a tree on the hillside and took a seat. Her head throbbing and stomach churning, she looked down at her watch once more. *8:39:16. I suppose it wouldn't hurt if I closed my eyes for a few minutes.* Rolling her head back, Kate closed her eyes for the first time since arriving on the island.

4:13:44

The clouds had turned dark as the rain began to fall. Droplets descended upon the canopy and echoed the beating sounds of a downpour. Drips began to find their way through as they fell to the forest floor. Kate awoke to the sensation of droplets on her forehead. Stretching and looking up, she quickly realized the feeling was real. Alert, she wiped her forehead and looked down at her watch. *Dammit.*

Kate slowly began to stand up, her boots skidding in the mud; she grabbed the nearby tree for support. Wiping her hands and knees, she grabbed the bow and arrows and continued north down the hill, paying careful attention to her footing. *I still have plenty of time. I can get there with over an hour to spare.* The rain continued to fall on the canopy; small streaks of water fell through the openings. Looking forward, she began to make out the bottom of the hill. "Almost there," she said to herself.

As she rounded the tree, an arrow whisked through the air and struck the trunk inches from her hand. Completely startled, Kate fell backward onto the ground. She wiped her face as she turned and looked back up the hill. *Nothing.* She took a deep breath, trying to remain calm.

"Weetwooh," a voice whistled from above.

Kate continued to survey the hill, now certain she wasn't alone. *Who is it this time?*

Emerging from behind a tree uphill, Mr. Black rolled around with a scowl on his face as he prepared to fire his bow a second time.

Kate sat there in shock; she was convinced Mr. Black had died in the field. *How is he still alive?* Not having time to weigh her options, she quickly grabbed her bow, drew and fired. The arrow soared up the hill and missed Mr. Black by several feet. He turned to watch the arrow glide to a stop at the base of a nearby tree.

Turning his attention back to Kate, he fired a second arrow. It landed directly between her legs. "That's enough, Kate. Fire again, and I won't miss next time," he began. "Toss that bow away."

Kate looked down at the bow, and then to the arrow in the dirt between her feet. *If he was planning to shoot me, he'd have done it already.* Looking back up at Mr. Black, who had begun to slowly descend the hill toward her, she clutched the bow and tossed it to her left, several feet out of reach.

"Excellent decision, sweetheart," Mr. Black continued. "And how was your nap? You looked so peaceful, I couldn't bear to wake you. I hope your batteries are good and charged for what happens next." Mr. Black halted his march a few feet from Kate.

Kate got to her feet and looked around. She was covered in mud and debris as the rain continued to fall. Getting a good look at Mr. Black, blood ran down his face from a bright red tear in his cheek. Kate continued to stare at the wound as Mr. Black touched it with his finger, and then examined the blood that came off.

"I'll tell you one thing," he began, "I never expected you to get the jump on me like that." He wiped his bloody finger on his pants. "Imagine if you actually knew how to properly shoot one of these things." He held the bow up for Kate to see.

"You didn't exactly leave me any choice. So, what happens now?" Kate said while standing her ground.

"We finish this," Mr. Black said as he came up and pushed Kate backward off her feet and down the hill.

Kate rolled and tumbled in the mud for several rotations until a tree broke her fall. Quickly reacting to the blow, she got to her knees and looked up the hill. Mr. Black was casually strutting down to her. Wasting no time, she got to her feet, turned, and began to run down the hill. Ducking below branches and darting between trees, Kate didn't have time to watch her steps as she sprinted toward the bottom. An arrow whisked passed her shoulder as she descended. In the distance, Mr. Black cursed at the miss.

Making the bottom of the hill and arriving on flat terrain, Kate quickly looked over her shoulder. Mr. Black was gone. Pausing for a moment, she glanced up the hill again and listened quietly. *Where are you?*

Turning her attention away from the hill, she continued north when a strong thrust struck her from the side and sent her tumbling. On her stomach, she rolled around in the mud and looked up at Mr. Black, who stood a few feet away, smiling as blood continued to run down his face. Pausing, he took off his backpack, set it on the ground, and then took his bow and tossed it several feet away. Looking down at his side he removed a knife and snapped it open.

Paralyzed by recent events, Kate stared at Mr. Black as he began to approach her. Needing to keep him back, she swung her legs. Easily dodging her attack, Mr. Black reached out and grabbed her boot in midair, took hold, and flung her back onto her stomach. "C'mon, Kate, you can do better," he said.

Kate quickly rolled face-up, but it was too late, as Mr. Black grabbed a handful of her hair and dragged her upright. "I've been looking forward to this all day." He smiled. "Though I was hoping for a little more of that fighting spirit from you." Mr. Black pulled her head closer to his.

In a last-ditch effort, Kate swung her fist at Mr. Black's face. He easily deflected the attack with his elbow. Looking him square in the eye, she spit in his face and lunged her forehead at his while attempted to swing her head free from his grip. He immediately let go of her hair and pushed her back while he wiped his face and rubbed his forehead from the unexpected impact. He glared at her with frustrated disapproval. Resetting his feet, Mr. Black lunged forward and drove the knife into Kate's left thigh.

Kate let out a scream as the knife pierced her leg. She had never felt a pain like this before, infinitely sharp and paralyzing. Mr. Black's strike was fast. Blood began to flow from her wound less than a second after Mr. Black removed the knife. Kate put both hands on the wound and attempted to apply pressure, though she knew it would do little good.

On his feet, Mr. Black rounded behind Kate, wiping the blade on his pants, and pressed her face-down into the mud with the back of his boot. "I owed you that one for the arrow earlier." He pointed toward his left cheek.

Kate continued to grimace and breathe heavily. Looking up from the mud, Mr. Black's backpack a few feet away. She began to crawl toward the bag.

"Now, where do you think you're going, sweetheart?" he said as Kate began to crawl for the bag. Smiling, Mr. Black didn't follow, as he stood and played with the knife. "Do whatever it is you want, but I can promise you one thing, you're about to die much, much worse than your friend Chris did."

Kate didn't respond, nor did she change course. Kicking and crawling through the mud, she reached for the bag.

"The bow isn't over there," he said.

Diving her arm into his bag, she began to fish around inside. Where are you?

"And when I'm done here," Mr. Black said as he began to advance, "I think I'll go pay Mr. Wu a visit. Can't wait to see the look on his face when he hears about this."

Found you. In a frantic motion, Kate withdrew her hand from the pack, gripping Mr. Black's flare gun.

Mr. Black froze.

"Neither can I," Kate responded as she aimed and pulled the trigger. In a blinding flash, the flare struck Mr. Black in the face and exploded. Mr. Black fell to the ground, dropping the knife and bringing his hands to his face in the process. Smoke rose from his flesh as he rolled in the mud and began to scream and moan.

Sitting up, Kate quickly crawled over, picking up his knife in the process. Mr. Black continued to scream as she arrived at his side. Rolling him onto his back, she climbed on top and straddled his chest. His left eye was irreparably damaged, and his hairline was burnt back several inches. His hair continued to emit smoke as the rain fell on them both.

Kate looked down upon Mr. Black, feeling zero empathy or hesitation. He stared back at her in terror with his remaining eye. Slowly bringing his hands open and to the side of his head, Mr. Black began to speak. Before words could come out of his mouth, Kate raised the knife and repeatedly drove it down into his chest. Mr. Black didn't resist as he took his last gasps. Pausing, she tossed the bloody knife away and stared down at Mr. Black as his life faded away. "For Chris," she said as she dismounted Mr. Black's body and sat in the mud.

Kate looked up at the treetops as the rain continued to fall, and blood continued to rush from her leg. The pain was excruciating. She knew time was running short. But all she could do at that moment was look back at Mr. Black's body as she began to cry. She didn't move for several moments, her eyes transfixed on Mr. Black as she wiped rain, mud, and tears from her face.

As she continued to lean forward, a hand softly touched her shoulder. Still very alert, Kate swung around, ready for a second bout. Hesitating, she looked up to see Ranger standing over her. Reaching down, he offered her his hand. "Can you walk?" he said as the rain beaded down on his safari hat.

2:12:41

R anger trudged through the trees, marching slowly to the north with Kate hanging over his shoulder. The knife wound to her leg left Kate unable to safely navigate the terrain, nor was she likely to survive much longer if she kept losing blood. She had initially insisted on walking to the extraction herself, but after a few hundred yards, she had succumbed to the pain and collapsed against a tree. She reluctantly accepted Ranger's offer to carry her north. After carefully wrapping her leg, Ranger threw her over his shoulder and began his march. Neither said a word to the other.

0:13:22

anger sat Kate down in the grass. Waves crashed against the dock behind her. The terrain was mostly flat, the sea surrounding her from behind, and the vastness of trees and mountainous hills in front of her.

"Have you seen Kevin?" she asked Ranger, who continued to stand next to her and look at his watch.

"I have not," he replied without breaking his glance.

"Do you know if he's alive? Do you know where he is?" Kate wasn't in the mood for short answers as her leg and head continued to throb.

"I'm sorry Kate, I'm not at liberty to discuss your friend," Ranger said with a sigh.

After a short pause, Kate looked up at Ranger a second time. "Do I get to leave? Is it over?"

He looked away from his watch and knelt next to her. "In ten minutes and twelve seconds, you get to go home." He smiled and examined her leg. "In all my years out here, I must say, that was quite the performance."

Kate said nothing as she watched him inspect her wound.

He looked up at her and smiled. "You'll definitely need some stitches, and possibly surgery, but you'll be just fine." He stood and began to pace in the grass.

"What happens to the bodies?"

"We'll take care of them."

"And how will their deaths be explained?" she continued.

"We always have contingencies."

Realizing she wasn't going to get much information from Ranger, Kate looked up at the sun shining down on her face; the clouds and rain had cleared out during the hike from the woods.

In the distance, flapping rotor blades of a helicopter grew louder. To her right, a small black object took form. She stared at the object for several minutes until it came into full view and began to slow its approach. The helicopter roared overhead as it swung around for a landing in the clearing just to her left.

Kate stared down at her watch as the final seconds ticked away. 5....4....3....2...1. The watch vibrated a few times, and then the screen went dark. Looking up, she watched as the helicopter touched down in the field. The breeze from the rotor blades flung her hair back as Ranger walked up to the pilot and gave him a thumbs up.

Turning around, Ranger made his way to Kate and helped her to her feet, and they slowly walked to the helicopter. Opening the door, Ranger helped Kate in and fastened her belt. He looked up at Kate and gestured for her to wait 'one minute' as Ranger walked to the front of the helicopter and out of sight.

The helicopter's blades continued to spin. Sitting nearby, she spotted a black headset with a microphone. Reaching over, she grabbed the headphones and put them on.

"Good afternoon," a voice said through the headset. Kate looked around. *It must be the pilot.* She began to talk, but the voice didn't respond. "You need to press the white switch on the cable if you want to talk."

Looking down, she found the toggle and flipped it up. "Does this work? Can you hear me?" she said.

"Loud and clear," the man replied. "Everything alright back there?

217

There's water in the compartment between the seats; help yourself."

Kate leaned over, opened the cooler, pulled out a chilled bottle of water, and began to chug.

"How was the weekend?" the man continued.

Kate wasn't sure how to respond. Was this a test? Was this man completely oblivious to what was happening? "A weekend I'll never forget," she said calmly.

"Well, that's just excellent," he added. "Anywho, we're waiting on one more person, and then we'll be shipping out. Shouldn't be but a few minutes."

Kevin! Kate began to look around for movement. It had to be Kevin; there was nobody else left. Eagerly waiting, Kate continued to look out every window she could in the hope of spotting movement.

Moments later, Ranger re-emerged with another man. Kate immediately recognized who Ranger was with: Mr. Blue. Ranger carefully helped him into the helicopter. Mr. Blue softly walked to the other side and took a seat. Kate stared at him with anxious hatred. Ranger stepped in next, closing the door behind him, and made his way to Mr. Blue. Similar to what he did with Kate, Ranger strapped Mr. Blue in and handed him a headset, and then pounded on the wall of the cockpit as he took a seat.

Kate stared at Mr. Blue as the helicopter lifted. He had clearly received attention; he was sporting new clothing, his head was cleaned and bandaged, and his arm was in a sling. Mr. Blue stared back at Kate and smiled. Neither broke eye contact until well after the helicopter had cleared land. Kate looked to her left out the window as the island shrank below. The sun was beginning to set over the western hills, and all was uncomfortably still from up above.

"Pity about your friend," Mr. Blue said with a grin on his face.

Kate looked back at Mr. Blue, then shifted her attention. "Where's Kevin?" Kate said, directing her attention toward Ranger.

Ranger didn't say a word. "Kevin won't be joining us, I'm afraid," Mr. Blue replied.

"What does that mean?"

"He's no longer with us."

"What?" Kate said as she stared back at Ranger.

"I'm afraid it's true," Ranger said, finally speaking up.

Taking a short pause, she glared at Mr. Blue, who continued to smile. "You son of a bitch!" Kate attempted to jump from her chair toward Mr. Blue, but Ranger immediately grabbed her and put her back in her seat.

"Think you might do us all a favor and open that door," Mr. Blue said to Ranger, "then toss her out."

"Why don't you come over here and give it a try? Worked so well the last two times," Kate quickly responded.

"Enough! Both of you," Ranger shouted as he spread his arms to keep Kate and Mr. Blue apart. "The game is over. In fact, if either one of you lays a hand on each other, I'll take Mr. Blue up on his suggestion and throw your ass out the door. Do I make myself clear?" Ranger stared back and forth between Kate and Mr. Blue. They both nodded.

***

The helicopter continued to swiftly fly over the water. Nearly an hour had elapsed, and nobody had said a word since the initial verbal jousting at takeoff. Kate caught Ranger speaking into his microphone a few times, though she couldn't hear a word and assumed he was talking to somebody on a different frequency.

Mr. Blue hadn't moved all flight. He stared forward or out the window and didn't attempt to speak to Ranger again. Though, Kate did catch him looking over at her a few times. *Please try and make a move.*

"Alright, Kate," Ranger said as he broke the silence, "we're almost there. For security purposes, I need you to put this on." Ranger handed

Kate a black bag.

Kate took the bag in her hands. "You've got to be kidding."

"I'm afraid not," Ranger said as he stared intently at her.

"Well, what about him?" Kate pointed toward Mr. Blue.

"Don't worry about him, he's already signed his life away," Ranger continued while turning his gaze on Mr. Blue, and then back to Kate. "I need you to comply."

Kate stared at Ranger for a few seconds and then nodded. Opening the black bag, she slowly placed it over her head.

III

The Tiebreaker Protocol

Chapter 44

Kate was seated firmly in a cushy chair when the bag was finally lifted from her face. It took her eyes a second to adjust as she looked around a large room with animal trophies mounted on the walls. A dark man with glasses sat at a desk in front of her. To her left, Mr. Blue was sitting in a similar chair; he didn't turn to make eye contact. Behind the desk stood a large stone fireplace with a fire burning fresh timber.

Kate continued to look around, not daring to be the one to break the silence. Behind her stood two burly men in white jackets. Over her left shoulder, Ranger sat in a chair against the wall, his gaze transfixed on a book in his hand. She returned her gaze to the dark man as the wood fire crackled.

"I must say," the dark man began, "it's nice to finally meet you in person, Miss Alan."

"And who are you?" she responded politely.

"I am the Broker," he replied with a nod.

"And why am I here?"

"Great question, Miss Alan," the Broker said as he pushed back his chair, stood, and rounded the desk toward her. "At first, bringing you here was part of standard operating procedure. It's been some time since one of our prey actually survived an excursion." He stopped and braced his weight on the corner of the desk and continued. "Truth be told, we were planning to have a little chat, have you sign some paperwork, and then send you on your way."

Kate rolled her eyes. "And let me guess, something has come up?"

"How apt you are, Miss Alan," the Broker said as he pointed his index finger at her, stood, and began walking back to his chair. "It was brought to our attention just before you took off from the island that Mr. Blue here had issued a challenge."

Kate looked over at Mr. Blue, who was now glaring at her.

"Mr. Blue is claiming his disqualification and subsequent dealings with Mr. Ranger inhibited his ability to finish the competition."

Kate cackled and looked over again at Mr. Blue, who continued to stare at her with a straight face.

"Something funny, Miss Alan?" the Broker asked.

"I'm just surprised Mr., uh, Blue here would make that claim."

"And why do you say that?"

"Because the last time I saw him, he could barely walk, and had an arrow through his arm."

"An arrow you put there," Mr. Blue snapped.

Kate turned her gaze to Mr. Blue and smiled. "I sure did."

"Regardless of that fact," the Broker interjected, "the judges have reviewed his claim and determined he would have had a fifty-two percent chance of defeating Mr. Wu in hand-to-hand combat and eventually returning to the competition, where he could have, in fact, won the expedition. Especially considering with the leg wound you suffered during your bout with Mr. Black."

Kate stood and planted her hands on the desk. She grimaced from the shooting pain of her leg injury. "He didn't kill Kevin?"

"Most certainly not, Miss Alan. Please sit," the Broker replied while glaring at her.

"Then what happened to him? Where is he?"

"Ask Mr. Ranger, he was there," the Broker said as he leaned in.

"Miss Alan, I'm not going to ask again," he added while gesturing for her to sit.

Kate sat back in her chair, taken aback.

"Do you want to tell her, or should I?" the Broker shouted over to Ranger.

"Go right ahead," Ranger mumbled back without taking his gaze from his book; he appeared clearly agitated by the current events.

"As it turns out, in his pursuit of Mr. Blue here, Mr. Wu stumbled upon a plaque that provided specific details toward the previous ownership of the island and its whereabouts."

"So, you killed him?" Kate asked.

The Broker paused and then made eye contact with Kate. "It's quite unfortunate that Mr. Wu stumbled upon the plaque; it was an unexpected turn of events. Nevertheless, countermeasures had to be enacted."

"Countermeasures?"

"I'm sorry, Miss Alan, you will never see Mr. Wu again." The Broker sat back in his chair and adjusted his glasses.

Kate fell silent. *Chris is dead. Who knows what they'll do to Kevin? And I'm not getting out of here alive.*

"Now, to the matter at hand," the Broker continued. "As I was saying, our judges reviewed Mr. Blue's claim and sided with him in a vote of 3-2."

"That's great news," Mr. Blue interjected.

"Please wait a moment, Mr. Blue," the Broker interrupted. "Though the judges agreed with your claim, probabilities were also run on Miss Alan here, who, as we all know, disposed of Mr. Black. It was determined that Miss Alan, even with her injury, had a clear advantage over you in hand-to-hand competition, and you did not have a significant enough advantage over her in using weapons."

Mr. Blue leaned forward and interrupted, "You can't be serious!"

"It is the determination of our judges that a victory for either of you was within the margin of error," the Broker continued. "As such, we are going to exercise the Tiebreaker Protocol."

Kate looked over at Mr. Blue, who was clearly furious at the decision. "And what's the tiebreaker protocol?" she asked.

"Let's find out," the Broker said as he opened a side drawer of his desk, reached in, and removed a manila envelope. He quickly inspected the envelope to ensure it hadn't been tampered with and then leaned forward and grabbed the letter opener that sat on the desk a few feet in front of Kate. The Broker slit the envelope, broke the seal, and opened the top. Reaching inside, he removed a single piece of paper and placed it in front of himself. Leaning forward, he placed the letter opener back.

The Broker reviewed the letter in detail for several moments, and then lifted his attention to Kate and Mr. Blue, who sat and silently waited. The Broker smiled and put the paper down on the desk. "Well, this is an interesting scenario. Though I find it similar to a game of football where two sides engage in a ninety-minute battle of skill and strategy only for the game to be settled by a shootout where a person has to defend a giant net against a skilled opponent, this feels strangely fitting for you two." The Broker opened a drawer to his right and removed a small revolver from the drawer and set it down on the table. Reaching back in, he carefully removed a single bullet and set it on the desk next to the gun.

Kate and Mr. Blue sat silently in shock.

"Five chambers, one bullet," the Broker continued. "We go until there's a winner."

"Absolutely not," Mr. Blue fired back. "I didn't give you seventeen million dollars so I could play a bout of Russian roulette against an unremarkable grad student."

The Broker sat silently, his fingers crossed. "Then you forfeit your claim, Miss Alan wins, and you both go home."

"I'd rather die!" Mr. Blue shouted as he looked over at Kate.

"So, then we're playing?"

Mr. Blue looked over at Kate, who appeared amused by his frustrations. "You're damn right we are," Mr. Blue concluded.

The Broker calmly grabbed the gun, opened the loader, placed the bullet inside, and snapped the gun shut. He looked over at Mr. Blue and began to hand him the pistol. "Mr. Blue is challenging the current outcome, as such, it's his honor." He handed Mr. Blue the revolver. "Under the chin, please," the Broker added.

Mr. Blue looked down at the gun. Calmly he brought the revolver under his chin, cocked the gun, took a deep breath, closed his eyes, and pulled the trigger.

Click.

He sighed, exhaling slowly, and smiled as he handed the gun back to the Broker. The Broker accepted the weapon and immediately made his way to Kate and handed the gun to her.

"I'm not touching that," Kate said as she refused the gun.

The Broker paused in frustration and contemplated his next move.

"Take the gun, Kate," Ranger shouted from across the room. "One way or another, you will play until they're satisfied."

She knew Ranger was right, and for some reason his demeanor had changed. She knew she couldn't count on his help anymore. Reaching forward, she reluctantly accepted the gun from the Broker. She looked down at the old gun in her lap; it was lighter than she expected. The metal was pristine, and the grip made of faded wood. Taking a deep breath, she cocked the gun, brought it to her chin, and pulled the trigger.

Click.

Relieved, she immediately tossed the gun back onto the desk before the Broker could reach her. She quivered at the sight of the gun and the unfathomable gamble she'd just made with her life. *I'm not doing that again.*

The Broker handed the gun back to Mr. Blue, who swiped it from his hand. Clearly, he had hoped for a single round. He looked down at the gun and hesitated. "Screw it," he said softly as he cocked the gun, raised it to his chin and pulled the trigger.

Click.

Kate immediately felt the rush; she wasn't sure if it was adrenaline or anxiety, but she knew the deck was no longer in her favor. She stared motionless at the desk as Mr. Blue handed the Broker the gun. The Broker looked down at the gun, wiped it with his sleeve, and then gave it to Kate, who accepted without breaking her gaze. She didn't move or speak.

"Miss Alan," the Broker said as he interrupted her gaze, "it's your turn." He sat back in his chair and watched intently.

Kate knew what she had to do; it was the only way she would get out of there alive. She looked down at the gun and cocked the trigger. She smiled and brought it up beneath her chin. She looked over at Mr. Blue and smiled. "No rules, am I right?" She looked back at the Broker and closed her eyes.

Taking a deep breath, Kate lowered her arm, pointed the gun at the Broker and pulled the trigger. The gun immediately fired and recoiled. The bullet struck the Broker in the shoulder as he fell back in his chair and began to wail. Leaning forward, Kate grabbed the letter opener from the desk and, in a pivoting swing, drove it into Mr. Blue's neck. Everything happened so fast, Mr. Blue hadn't moved from his seat. Kate stood there and held the letter opener in his neck as life faded from his eyes. Blood squirted out over his clothing and all over her face. His knuckles were white as he made clawing fists at Kate, who stood over him smiling as blood continued to squirt.

"Aw, hell," Ranger said as he stood and gestured to the men in white at the back of the room, who were already moving in on Kate, "get that from her."

The two men quickly grabbed Kate and freed her grip from the letter opener, which was still in Mr. Blue's neck. Grabbing her from both sides, they pushed her to her knees. She didn't put up a fight. *Whatever happens now, happens. For the first time since this all began, I'm doing this on my terms.* She continued to smile and stare at Mr. Blue's body. Ranger approached her from the side, and after a small pinch behind her ear, the room faded into black.

IV

Aftermath

Chapter 45

Inhaling deeply, Kate anxiously woke and sat up in one motion. Her vision was a bit blurry, but she could see she was in a room. Looking down, she ran her hand across a tapestry she knew; it was her comforter. With her eyes coming to focus, she looked around to confirm her suspicion. *How did I get to my apartment?*

She pushed back the blankets and looked down at her leg. Her thigh was bruised but neatly held together with stitches and Dermabond, and covered with a white bandage. The wound was sore to the touch, but she had clearly received care from a medical professional. She had no memory after killing Mr. Blue, but knew somebody had brought her home and treated her injury. Raising her hand, she gazed at a second set of bandages on her wrist where the countdown watch used to reside. Peeling an edge of the bandages away, she could see a small incision on the inside of her wrist. *Interesting.*

Bewildered, Kate silently got out of bed and limped to her bedroom door. Cars honked on the streets below. The light streamed in through the edges of her window. On her shelf, the clock read 11:42. She grabbed the robe hanging on the back of her desk chair and flung the bedroom door open.

She tiptoed down the hallway into her kitchen. Everything was where it should be. She leaned over the kitchen counter and peered into her living room. Everything was as expected, except she spotted her camping pack leaning against the wall near her front door.

Buzz. Buzz.

Startled, she looked down the counter at her cell phone as it vibrated and flickered. She calmly walked over and answered.

"Hello?"

"Hello, Miss Kathryn Alan, please," a woman's voice said on the other line.

"Speaking."

"Good morning, Miss Alan, this is Christina over at D&G Bank, just calling to confirm your appointment for this morning?" the voice continued.

Kate scratched her head, "Uh, when was it again?"

"Right now, that's why we're calling, we wanted to make sure we were still on."

"And what's the nature of today's meeting?" Kate hadn't the faintest idea, though it was most likely related to her ballooning student loans the bank had financed.

"It's regarding the lump-sum deposit that hit your account yesterday, don't you remember? We were going to discuss your allocations."

Deposits? Kate looked up at the clock. She was curious what was going on, and the last thing she needed was a disruption to her loans right before classes resumed. "I'll be there in five minutes."

"Excellent, see you then, Miss Alan."

Kate hung up and walked back to her bedroom to find suitable clothes. D&G Bank was three blocks from Kate's apartment. She slipped on a pair of jeans and a comfortable top and headed out the door.

Several minutes later, Kate limped into D&G Bank and asked for Christina, who quickly came from one of the side offices to greet and chauffer her back to her office.

"I'm so glad you've chosen us, Miss Alan," Christina began as she sat down behind her desk. "I've been personally assigned to manage your account moving forward."

"I'm not entirely sure that's necessary," Kate replied as she sat down, resting her hand softly on her tender thigh.

"You don't have to be modest with us, Miss Alan, and do you prefer that? Or, may I call you Kate?" Christina continued.

"Kate is fine."

"Great. Well, Kate, as you requested, we put together a preliminary investment portfolio. Diversified to your specifications, of course, and I thought we could maybe start there?"

Kate had no clue what she was talking about. "Are you sure you have the right Kate?"

"Well, I don't know, can you please hand me your driver's license and I'll pull up your accounts?"

Kate reached into her purse, yanked out her driver's license and handed it to Christina.

Christina began to type and look at the screen. Moments later, she printed a piece of paper. "Everything looks fine," she said while handing Kate her license back. Pivoting around in the chair, she pulled a piece of paper from the printer and placed it in front of Kate. "See, your balances are in order, we just need to know where you want to put them."

Kate leaned forward and gazed at the document. Her heart fluttered. She made a fist under the desk and blinked a few times to make sure she was reading the document correctly.

```
Checking Account Balance .............. $40,802,411.67
Savings Account Balance ............... $16,436.62
```

"Everything alright, Miss Alan, I mean, Kate?" Christina asked.

Coughing as she tried to speak, Kate paused and took a deep breath. "Yes, I'm fine."

"You sure?" Christina leaned in and looked her over carefully. "'Cause you're looking a little pale. Do you want me to get you some water?"

Kate's heart continued to flutter as she tried to make eye contact with Christina and use her words, but she couldn't keep her eyes off the sheet of paper nestled between her hands. Deep down, she had the feeling something was terribly wrong with these fortuitous events. Feeling the pulsing throb in her knee as her heart continued to race, she never lost sight of the island in her mind. *No way this is a coincidence.*

"Miss Alan?"

Looking up, Kate was lost in thought and forgot the question. "I'm sorry? Wait, yes, water. I mean, no, I don't need any water. Thank you." She needed to get her eyes elsewhere. Leaning forward she took the piece of paper, folded it into eighths, and placed it in her pocket.

Christina stared at her for a moment, slightly puzzled by Kate's borderline erratic reaction. Wasting no time, she spun around in her chair to the large green filing cabinet behind her desk. Opening the bottom drawer, she thumbed through a series of gray tagged files. Reaching down, she drew one from the drawer. "Here we are." Turning around to face Kate, she placed the folder on the desk. "If you'd like to continue, we have some investment recommendations I'd like to share with you."

"Sounds great," Kate said as she took a deep breath and leaned forward.

Chapter 46

K ate quickly returned home from the bank but stopped along the way at her favorite local cafe, The Emporium LTD. She never quite understood the 'limited' part of the name, but the coffee more than made up for any ambiguity. She got the cup to-go and quickly rounded the corner and made her way home.

Walking in her front door, Kate had already pulled the folded bank statement from her pocket and continued to reexamine. *Forty million dollars. How do I even begin to explain this?* She turned and shut the door behind her and made her way to the kitchen.

"Hello, Kate," a familiar voice said as Kate jumped back in complete surprise. Her eyes had been on the bank statement, her mind elsewhere, and she didn't even manage to notice Ranger sitting in her living room rocking chair. "Sorry to startle you, I wasn't sure you'd even notice me if I didn't speak up." He smiled at her. "No reason to worry, you are perfectly safe, I'm only here to discuss a few loose ends."

Kate stood against the wall, very surprised to see Ranger again. "How did you..."

"Please have a seat," he interrupted while kindly gesturing for her to sit on the couch adjacent to the rocking chair. Around the room, everything appeared in order, except for the TV, which was on a news channel and muted. Looking directly at Ranger, she pushed back from the wall, gently rounded the couch, and took a seat as far from Ranger as possible.

"I see you've been to the bank," he added with a smile.

"Was this you?" she asked while waving the bank statement in the air.

"Not only me," he said as he continued to smile. There was a long pause. Kate anxiously sat at the end of the couch, trying to break eye contact with Ranger, who sat politely and didn't move as he gazed upon Kate. "You sure surprised everyone, Kate. It was one thing to get off the island in one piece, but what you pulled at the estate shocked all of us."

"You told me on the helicopter it was over," she replied.

"Indeed I did, and I thought that was the case," Ranger replied. "I didn't learn of the challenge until we were almost back to the estate. I'm really sorry about all of that; I disagreed with the panel regarding the legitimacy of the challenge. Alas, I was overruled."

Kate stared at Ranger and didn't move or say a word.

Ranger looked down at the statement in Kate's hands. "The funds reflect the purse in its entirety from the weekend," he continued. "The judge panel, along with myself, hope you'll accept it as a gesture of goodwill."

"And it's not because everybody else is dead?" Kate interrupted.

"That certainly plays a part in it. Truth be told, we underestimated you. We knew you had the skills and athleticism to hold your own out there, but before our eyes, you transformed into someone else entirely."

Kate leaned forward and made sharp eye contact with Ranger. "That's what happens when you kidnap people and hunt them like animals," she replied. "I mean, who the hell do you people think you are? Just because your clients have money and power doesn't mean they can literally prey on others."

"That's only in some scenarios," he interrupted. "APEX offers a variety of entertainment options; you were simply unfortunate enough to be part of one of our classic expeditions."

"You know what, I should call the police right this second." Reaching down, she began to pull the phone from her pocket.

"We both know that won't do you any good."

Kate paused and held the phone in her hand.

"Think about it. We found you, evaluated you, lifted your entire crew without leaving a trace. We flew you several thousand miles around the face of the globe, dropped you in our expedition, and nobody was the wiser. I promise you we've been doing this for a very long time, and our clients pay us very well to run a tight ship."

"You're still facilitating the killing of innocent people for sport. What about Chris? What about Kevin? They're never coming home, and what of their families?" Kate replied.

"What happened to your friends was very unfortunate, and I am genuinely sorry for your loss. But you're smart, you have a business background. These people are powerful, and they have built their lives on the backs of others; that's what funds the whole show. The only difference between what we do and the unholy slaughterhouse out there is our brand doesn't suck people dry for their entire adult lives. When our contestants come to APEX, they live, however brief it may be."

"I don't believe you buy that for a second," Kate replied. "You're nothing like them. What are you even doing working with these people?"

Ranger paused and looked down. "Everybody reports to somebody. I'm just fortunate enough to do something I'm good at."

"Rationalize your actions and theirs all you want, you're all still wrong."

Ranger paused and looked up at Kate. He didn't respond, and from Kate's read of the situation, he wasn't going to bite.

"So, where do we go from here?"

"That, Kate, is entirely up to you," Ranger replied as he moved toward her. "You have killed two people, you have forty million in your bank account, and we're never far away." He reached down, turned over her bandaged wrist, and softly tapped the spot of the incision. "It's harmless, and medical experts will never find it, but you're now in this game for life." He softly let go of her hand and began to walk to the kitchen. Kate didn't move. "Oh," he continued as he turned toward Kate, "you might find this next piece particularly interesting." He pointed the remote and unmuted the TV. Kate turned to watch.

"...And over the weekend, a harrowing turn of events left one local businessman dead, and another injured," the newscaster began. "We now turn to Holly with the full report. Take it away, Holly."

The TV shifted to video footage of a car on fire and rescue vehicles surrounded. A female voice began to speak. "A local businessman lost his life to a hit-and-run after stopping his vehicle to help rescue a man from the inferno of this vehicle. Here at RXBTV, we can confirm the man killed was local business owner Don Merrill, as shown here, who stopped his car to help get this man, Thomas Arthur, out of his burning vehicle."

Kate gasped as they flashed up the pictures of the two men on the screen. Don Merrill was Mr. Blue, and Thomas Arthur was the Broker. She looked over at Ranger, who was now in the kitchen fixing himself a glass of lemonade. "Hope you don't mind," he said as he filled the glass. Kate looked back at the TV.

"We now go live with Thomas Arthur." The Broker showed up on screen next to a reporter. His hair was frazzled, clothing completely different from what she remembered, and his arm was in a sling. *The same shoulder I shot him.* "Mr. Arthur, tell us what happened."

"It's really tough to explain; one minute I was seated and making headway toward my home, the next my car was on fire, and I was being pulled out of the vehicle by Mr. Merrill."

The reporter next to him nodded. "And what of Mr. Merrill?"

The Broker looked over at the reporter. "You know what happened, he was unexpectedly killed. It's tragic, what else is there to say?"

The reporter nodded at the Broker. "It was quite heroic, what he did," she added.

The Broker looked down, pretending to be broken up, and then faced the camera. "Without a doubt, and I can tell you one thing, whoever did this, this isn't over. You will be seeing me again." The Broker pointed at the screen. The visuals cut back to the news studio. "Thank you for that report, Holly..."

Ranger returned to the room and muted the TV as he sat back in the recliner. He smiled as he looked over at Kate, who was very surprised. "Don't worry about him, as far as the judge panel is concerned, this case is closed. The money is yours to keep. We're counting on you to exercise a little discretion, and I hope by now you understand what will happen if you don't." Ranger guzzled the glass of lemonade.

"And how would I even begin to explain the money in my account? Or, the fact that multiple people knew I was out camping with Kevin and Chris? Who have now mysteriously disappeared?"

Ranger smiled, opened up his jacket, removed an envelope from the inner pocket, and tossed it on the coffee table in front of Kate. "Hotel and airport surveillance cameras, as well as rental car and restaurant bills paid with your credit card, will confirm you were hundreds of miles away from where Kevin and Chris were camping." Leaning back, he set the lemonade glass on the table next to the chair, stood, and began walking to the door.

Kate didn't move from her spot as she watched him make his way to the front door.

"Can I ask you one question?" Kate said, breaking the silence.

Ranger turned and smiled at Kate. "Of course."

"Out of curiosity, when we landed, there was a red piece of paper that said if we survived thirty-six hours, we'd get a grand prize." Kate paused and looked intently at Ranger. "What was it?"

Ranger smiled. "That's a great question." He turned and opened the door. "Take care of yourself, Kate. I hope we never meet again," he said as he exited and closed the door behind him.

Kate looked back at the envelope on the table. Leaning forward, she swiped it from the surface and opened the top. She removed and unfolded a single piece of paper. After reading it over, she realized Ranger had buttoned up her end just as well as the TV broadcast she'd just witnessed.

```
LandRidge Resort & Casino, Las Vegas, NV

Earnings Statement:
Winner:  Kathryn Alan
Game:  Royal Flush Parlay
Bet:  $20
Draw Payout:  5,000 / 1
Blind Parlay Payout:  410/1 of Draw

Cards:
Draw:  10, Jack, Queen, King, Ace — Diamonds
Blind Parlay:  9 — Diamonds

Payout:  $41,000,000
Logged Pit Gratuity:  $200,000
Net Earnings:  $40,800,000*
*State and Local Taxes are due within 30 days.


Thank you for staying with us at the LandRidge Resort and
Casino. We look forward to your future stay at our
world-class resort and attractions.
```

About the Author

Tyler Micheal is a film and video game enthusiast seeking to bring a similar mix of excitement and pace to fiction. He lives in Clarence, NY with his wife and son. APEX is his debut novel.

Contact Information:

Tyler@tylermichaelbooks.com

You can connect with me on:
🌐 http://www.tylermichaelbooks.com
🐦 https://twitter.com/AuthorTMichael

CPSIA information can be obtained
at www.ICGtesting.com
Printed in the USA
LVHW051636130621
690122LV00012B/1587